"Listen, I know a goat when I see one. Why didn't
you just say you wanted to hand that fellow some
information, then turn him loose."

They were ... ... was well-
it a. What happened?" Ham demanded.

DOC SAVAGE GOES TO WAR!

They were involved in something extraordinary. It
was a little like trying to describe the Grand Canyon
to someone who had never heard of the place.

Doc hesitated to tell them in plain words how big it
was, knowing he would sound overdramatic, so
spectacular that it would be incredible. It would
sound too wild to say that the immediate course of
the war, the lives of innumerable men, the future of
European nations, depended on whether they caught
one man . . .

Bantam Books by Kenneth Robeson
Ask your bookseller for the books you have missed

THE
HATE GENIUS
A DOC SAVAGE® ADVENTURE
BY KENNETH ROBESON

THE HATE GENIUS

*A Bantam Book / published by arrangement with
The Condé Nast Publications, Inc.*

PRINTING HISTORY
*Originally appeared in Doc Savage Magazine January 1945
as* Violent Night

Bantam edition / June 1979

ISBN 0–553–12780–2

Published simultaneously in the United States and Canada

PRINTED IN THE UNITED STATES OF AMERICA

THE HATE GENIUS

I

It came as soon as he saw Lisbon. The feeling of being afraid. There had been fog, a slate-colored depressing fog around the Clipper during the last five hundred miles of flying; and the plane popped out of it suddenly into bright sunlight. And there directly below was their destination, Lisbon, the westernmost of Europe's capitals. With its white houses and colored tile roofs and parks and gardens, fronting on the Rada de Lisboa. With its eleven-by-seven mile lake made by the widening of the Tagus river.

He had expected to be afraid as soon as he saw Lisbon, and what he felt wasn't too bad, so he was relieved. Not much relieved, though.

The plane began circling. He suspected something was wrong.

Looking down, he could see the Castello de San Jorge on its rocky hill in the Alfama district. And suddenly he realized that he could recall with an unnatural clarity the exact appearance of the ancient Castello de San Jorge. There was no reason for such an abrupt and striking memory, except nerves. He frowned down at the old citadel, which dominated the Alfama section, containing one of the nastiest slums in Europe. There was no use kidding himself. Nerves. He *was* having the jitters. As badly as he had expected to have them.

The Clipper continued to circle. Then the control compartment door finally opened and the Captain—

1

on a land plane he would have been called the Pilot—came out with a worried expression.

"Mr. Savage," the Captain said. "They won't let us land at the lower end."

"What would happen if you went ahead and landed there anyway?"

"Their anti-aircraft batteries would fire on us."

He held back his irritation with difficulty—he had a biting impulse to shout his anger. He had directed the pilot to land on the remote end of the big, lake-like Rada de Lisboa, because he had hoped to get ashore unobserved at that point. He was disappointed because the Portuguese officials wouldn't let the plane land there. It was a small disruption of his plans, but it filled him with hot anger. Another sign of how much he was on edge.

"Go ahead and make a normal landing," he said.

"Yes, sir," the Captain said. "I'm sorry."

"Nothing to be sorry about. It's not your fault," he said, and the words had a harshness he didn't intend them to have. The Captain looked worried as he made his way back to the compartment. The Portuguese officials were being cranky. They must have had enough tricks pulled on them in the course of the war to make them impatient with everyone.

The Clipper shortly went into its procedure landing approach.

His ill luck continued when he stepped ashore. He turned up his coat collar and tried to hurry through the bright modern new American trans-Atlantic terminal building. He was recognized, however.

He could hear the word going around while they examined his credentials: "Es la Señor Savage!" That was in Spanish, but he heard it in Portuguese, also.

More attention, he thought sourly, than the leading bullfighter used to get before the war. But he was flattered, and embarrassed, too.

He soon discovered that they were sending for a

welcoming committee to be composed of persons of local consequence. He hurried to put a stop to that.

He told them he was leaving immediately, that he couldn't linger in Lisbon to be entertained, that he was most profoundly sorry, and knew they probably didn't believe him. But they were polite about it, and he bowed out of their company, entering the airways terminal manager's office. He got from the office to the street via a window.

He walked rapidly for two blocks, then hailed a taxicab, one of the type which manufactured its own propelling gas in a furnace affair which rode on the rear bumper and which was as likely as not to cough handfuls of sparks at the passengers.

"Drive to the Cidae Baixa," he told the driver, then settled back to watch out for sparks, and to wonder if there was a red-headed young man following him.

There was.

Not wishing to jump at conclusions—in his state of nerves, he could be imagining things—he had the puffing, smelling, spark-belching cab take him around several streets in Cidae Baixa, the lower town. He became certain the red-headed man was on his trail, and that the fellow was fairly adept at snooping.

He said, in Portuguese, "Driver, do you know the Hotel Giocare?"

The driver said he did.

He gave the driver an envelope and said, "I want you to take this to the Hotel Giocare. Drive with it to the Hotel Giocare, and wait outside with it. Do not give it to the hotel clerk. Just wait outside. Across the street from the Giocare is the Ciriegia Park, where you can wait. I will pay you."

The driver turned the envelope in his hands and frowned at it. The envelope was sealed. As a matter of fact, it contained Doc Savage's driving license, pilot certificate, a few courtesy cards, a commission in the New York police department, and some other matter. He had emptied his billfold of the litter and put it in the envelope for no other reason than that the billfold was getting stuffed. He had done this on the plane, so the envelope still had been in his pocket.

"What will you pay me?" the driver asked.

Doc Savage named an amount equal to the fare.

"No, it will cost you twice as much," the driver insisted, for evidently he had decided his passenger was one of the mysterious international gentlemen, secretive about their business, who had been plentiful in neutral Lisbon for a couple of years.

"All right," Doc said curtly. To punish the driver for being greedy, he carefully wrote down the man's name and identification and description, letting the fellow see him do it.

They went on. The streets were narrow, the corners sharp. He picked a sharp corner, and after they were around it, stepped hurriedly out of the car and ducked into the handiest doorway. His cab went on. The other machine, the one occupied by the red-headed man, was out of sight when he quit his own cab, but it popped into view a moment later, passing within hand-reach.

Doc got a thorough look at the red-headed man. The fellow was around forty, not large, but with an intense animal expression. He was dapperly dressed, with tan gloves and a cane. He was leaning forward, both gloved hands resting on the cane, staring at the cab he was following.

His hair was about the color of a freshly cut carrot. His lips had an expression that was not exactly a grin, more of an I-like-this-sort-of-thing twist. He was a complete stranger.

Doc Savage began walking toward a hostelry called the Chiaro di Luna. He wondered about the red-headed man as he walked, trying to figure out who the fellow might be, and frightening himself with some of the possibilities.

The red-headed young man had seemed so vital and enthusiastic about doing his following job. He was so damned hearty about it. Whoever and whatever he was, he liked his job, and a man with enthusiasm for this kind of work was dangerous.

The Hotel Chiaro di Luna was a gaudy, noisy hostelry where you could go without attracting much attention. The name meant, in Italian, moonlight, but something relative to a circus or carnival would have been more appropriate.

"Mr. Carlos Napolena calling to see Mr. Scimmia," Doc Savage told the clerk.

His name was not Carlos Napolena, and neither was Monk Mayfair named Mr. Scimmia. Monk Mayfair was Lieutenant Colonel Andrew Blodgett Mayfair, a chemist of great ability when he worked at it, which wasn't very often because he liked excitement.

"By golly!" Monk said heartily. "By golly, I'm glad you showed up."

Monk looked and acted as if he were mentally about ten years old, which was deceptive. It would also have been entertaining, but he frequently overdid it. He was short, wide, homely, hairy; he had more than a general resemblance to an amiable ape, and Doc Savage sometimes suspected he went out of his way to cultivate the mannerisms of one.

Ham Brooks was with Monk. Ham was a lawyer. Calling Ham a lawyer was somewhat like calling Buckingham Palace a house.

Monk Mayfair and Ham Brooks were members of a group of five who had worked with Doc Savage for a long time. They were his associates, his assistants.

He knew them quite well, and so he was immediately sure that something was bothering them. They were hiding something from him, he decided.

He was badly scared. Monk and Ham rarely deceived him, and never except for good and vital reason. He tossed his hat on a table, trying to be casual, and wondered if there was someone hiding in the room with trained and cocked pistols. A wild idea, of course. But he was sure something was amiss.

"You are doing all right by yourselves," he said.

He meant the room. It was a rich place, although it ran a little more to red velvet than select taste dictated.

Ham explained, "The snazzy jernt was Monk's idea. This suite until recently was occupied, we were told, by the Sultan of something-or-other and ten of his favorite wives. The minute Monk heard that, nothing would do but that we should put up here."

Doc asked, "Who is paying for it?"

"Monk."

Monk's financial condition was pretty continuously one of being strapped. At Lisbon prices, the suite was rich for his purse.

"Paying with what?" Doc asked idly, still wondering what was wrong with Monk and Ham, puzzled about their uneasiness.

Monk said quickly, "I'm two-bit rich for a change. I sold a chemical formula to a fellow."

"A formula for making non-rubber baby pants," Ham said.

Monk winced. "I don't think it's so funny. I got paid for it."

Doc Savage took a deep breath and faced them.

"All right now," he said. "What is worrying you two fellows?"

They looked at him too innocently.

Watching them, his own uneasiness crawled up like a nest of snakes and frightened him additionally. He could not guess what might be wrong.

They had not, he was sure, been in Lisbon more than a day. When he had cabled them, they were in London, and he was in New York. His cable had instructed them to go immediately to Lisbon, to the Chiaro di Luna hotel, and wait for his appearance. That was all he had told them. He did not dare tell them anything more, even in code. He couldn't take chances with this matter.

He began to get angry. It is always a short step from tight nerves to rage. He scowled at them.

"Stop it!" he said. "You're behaving like kids!"

Monk and Ham looked so uncomfortable that he was ashamed of his harshness. He watched them, and he was sure that they were going to confess whatever was worrying them, but it would take a little time for them to get around to it.

He waited, and he thought again of the red-headed stranger. The thought of the fellow made him jump up, and on his feet he realized how jittery he was becoming. He went to the window and stared out, seeing the people in the street, the hucksters, the country folk from Almada and Sixal, the fishermen from Trafaria.

Monk finally spoke.

"Pat is here," Monk said.

Doc Savage wheeled. The news was so much different from anything he had expected. He almost laughed, yet he wasn't pleased.

"Lord!" he said. "Oh, Lord!"

Explanations and alibis poured out of Monk and Ham. "She was in London," Monk said. "She came over on a war correspondent's clearance she had wangled out of some magazine. They wouldn't—the military people wouldn't—let her go across and see action, so you can guess what Pat did. She told everybody from Eisenhower on down what she thought of them. So they jerked her credentials, except for a one-way pass back to New York. Pat refused to return to New York, so she was stranded in London."

Ham said, "We hid from her, Doc. Honest we did. But she vamped some somebody in the Intelligence office into giving her our address. So she found us. She found us a few hours before we got your message to come to Lisbon."

Monk spread his hands. "You know what happened. She found out you had assigned us a job—and came along."

"Why did you tell her about the cablegram?" Doc demanded.

"We didn't. She found it out. She's a mind-reader."

Ham said defensively, "She has never seen the cable. We destroyed it before she got her hands on it."

Doc frowned at them. "How on earth did she get from England to Portugal in times like these when she didn't have credentials."

"I don't know, but I think she let them think she was returning to New York by plane, and got herself routed through Lisbon."

"Anyway, she's here?"

"Yes."

"Where?"

"I'll get her," Monk said sheepishly. "She's got a room down the hall."

"Wait a minute," Doc said. He went into the bedroom of the suite, threw up a window he found there, and examined a convenient fire escape. "Come on," he said. "We're going to skip without seeing Pat."

Monk grinned. "I wish I could be around to hear what she has to say about it."

"Better get our clothes," Ham said. "Or are we coming back here?"

"Grab what you'll need," Doc said.

Ham and Monk did some hasty scooping of garments into a handbag, and Ham climbed out on the fire escape. Monk followed him, then Doc.

They went down two floors and there was a clattering uproar and a crash as a champagne bottle fell off a window sill, hit the areaway below and broke.

"Blazes!" Monk said. "Somebody had a thread stretched across—"

Pat Savage put her head out of a window above and said, "That's right, Monk. A thread. And guess who put it there."

II

Most males would admit that looking at Patricia Savage was an experience. She was a cousin of Doc Savage, a distant one, but she had some of the family characteristics which made Doc a striking figure. She had his height, and his remarkable bronze hair, and she had—almost—the strange flake-gold eyes which were Doc's outstanding peculiarity of appearance. She was something to be shown in kodachrome.

"I won't laugh at you," she told them. "But it's an effort not to."

Monk asked sourly, "How'd you know we would sneak out by the fire escape?"

"I figured that as soon as you told Doc I was here, he would get some such impulse," she said. "What's going on?"

"Going on?"

"Now, now, don't keep me in suspense," Pat told him. "And don't beat around the bush. Why did you rush to Lisbon? Why did Doc rush to Lisbon? What is it this time?"

"I don't know," Monk said. "And that's the truth. Doc hasn't taken time to tell us anything."

"But something is in the pot?"

"Of course."

They had returned to the sinful-looking velvet interior of the suite which Monk and Ham occupied. Monk and Ham skidded their handbags into the bedroom, and waited for Doc and Pat to have a

9

row. Doc would come out loser, they surmised, but it should be interesting to listen to.

Doc Savage lodged himself in a chair. He knew Monk and Ham expected to hear a row, and he knew Pat expected him to start one, and he decided to fool them. He wouldn't have an argument with Pat.

He looked thoughtfully at the floor. And in a moment his fears and his nervousness wrapped around him like a clammy blanket. His mood became like something from a grave.

Ten thousand curses, he thought gloomily, upon whatever it was that made Pat like dangerous excitement. Pat was okay. She was lovely. She was so beautiful she made men foolish, and she had brains. He wished to God she would marry some nice guy and mastermind him into becoming President, or something.

If only she hadn't come to Lisbon. Her presence here horrified him, because he knew the extent of the danger.

He was half tempted to tell her what she was getting into, just for the satisfaction of scaring the devil out of her. He smothered the impulse, because it would do no good. It would scare Pat stiff, but she would string along with the thing because of that crazy yen she had for dangerous excitement.

"I'm going to fool you," he told her. "I'm going to let you in on our little party without an argument."

She looked at him suspiciously. "Don't you feel all right?" she asked. "I mean, this doesn't sound like you."

"Would you go back to New York if I asked you to?" he demanded.

"I would not!"

"All right, I won't argue," he said. "I just give up. Stay if you want to."

She stared at him intently, trying to read him.

"You're scared," she decided. "Doc, you're scared. This is, I think, the first time I ever saw you plain out and out funked. You're just so plain darn terrified that you don't feel like arguing with me."

He nodded and said heavily, "That's right."

He could tell that she was shocked, that she was beginning to get scared herself.

"Why are we in Lisbon?" she demanded. "What is this, anyhow?"

He decided not to tell her now. There were several reasons for not doing so. There might be a microphone in the room, for one thing. The main reason was that he had, actually, not the slightest intention of letting Pat get involved in the affair. He couldn't think of a way now of bustling her off to New York, but he hoped to. In the meantime, he would keep her from finding out anything.

He said, "The man is a little less than average size, ruddy complexion, a few freckles, a grin like a man about to bite a baby. And red hair. The reddest hair you ever saw. Know him?"

"Not in my book," Monk said.

"I don't recall such a person," Ham said.

Pat looked interested. "Does he laugh a lot when he talks, and tell corny gags now and then? Seems to have a fancy cane and gloves to match every suit he wears?"

"About his talk I couldn't say, but he had brown gloves and a cane," Doc admitted. "He got on my trail as soon as I stepped off the plane."

Pat said, "He must be a fellow who has been popping his eyes at me. Didn't seem like a bad egg."

"You met him?"

"He introduced himself."

"What seemed to be his business?"

"Monkey business, the same as most guys who introduce themselves to me," Pat said. "He didn't strike me as a bad character, although he gets you down with his jokes, and you have the feeling that he has more energy than he knows what to do with."

"Know anything definite about him?"

"No, I don't."

Doc frowned, and decided that they had better

take a look at his red-headed man to make sure it was the same one Pat knew. He told Monk, Ham and Pat how the carrot-top had followed him from the Clipper base, and explained the trick he had used to mislead the fellow. "The theory of the trick was that he will ask the cab driver where he left me, and the cab driver will sell him the information, then also sell him the fact that he, the driver, has an envelope which he was to keep and deliver to me later. The envelope isn't sealed, so they will immediately take a look at the contents, and find that the stuff seems important. So the red-headed man, to get back on my trail, will be watching the waiting cab driver in front of the Hotel Giocare." He added dubiously, "If it all works out right."

It did.

"That's my red-headed man," Pat said. "That's Full-of-Jokes."

The red-headed man was sprawled on the grass in Giriegia Park. He had spread newspapers out on the grass and was lying on them, making a pretense of contemplating a statue of Pedro IV, emperor of Portugal during the troublesome Miguelite war period.

The cab driver had parked at the curb about forty yards distant and was sitting on the runningboard of his vehicle lunching on a bottle of wine and a long loaf of bread.

"I'm sure," Pat said. "I'm positive that's the same red-headed fellow."

"What would happen if you walked up to him?" Doc asked.

"How do you mean?"

"Are you on good terms? Have you slapped him, or anything, the way you've been known to do?"

"Not yet," Pat said. "Although I've a hunch he's a fellow who could stand a little slapping. What have you got on your mind?"

Doc explained, "We might as well rake that fellow in now and see what he can tell us."

"Grab him, you mean?"

Doc nodded. "Walk up to him, Pat. Stroll him around the corner. We'll form a reception committee."

She said, "I'll try it," and went toward the red-headed man.

The red-headed man gave up contemplating the statue of Pedro IV and grinned at Pat. He sprang to his feet and did a sweeping bow, talked for a while with Pat, then began shaking his head.

Pat turned and pointed at the waiting cab. The red-headed man looked at the cab, and while he was doing that, Pat hit him over the head with an object which she took from her purse. The red-headed man sprawled down in the grass.

Monk said, astonished, "She knocked him cold!"

"That's Pat," Doc agreed. "As subtle as a ton of bricks."

Monk and Ham hurried to join Pat. Doc detoured past the cab to get his envelope from the driver, and to tell the driver, "You keep on doublecrossing people, and it will get you in trouble!" The driver looked frightened, and lost no time getting into his machine and leaving.

Doc joined Pat. "Why did you hit him like that?"

"He wouldn't go for a walk," Pat explained.

"Stretch him out and look concerned about him," Doc said. "If he starts to wake up, belt him again. I'll go find a cab."

He had to walk three blocks before he found a cab. Returning with the machine, he discovered that a small crowd of curious had gathered, including two policemen. "Our friend fainted," Pat was telling the cops blandly.

They carried the red-headed man to the cab, loaded him inside, and got in themselves. The onlookers followed them, giving advice.

Doc was glad when the cab got moving. "What did you hit him with?" he asked Pat.

"My six-shooter," she said.

"It's a wonder you didn't brain him. It was about as subtle as shooting a sparrow with a cannon."

Pat wasn't impressed.

Monk jerked off the red-headed man's brown gloves. The fellow's hands were lean and strong, but there was nothing unusual about them. Monk was disappointed. "Thought he might be wearing gloves to cover up a scar or birthmark or something."

Pat began going through the red-headed man's clothing. She found quite a lot of money—paper money and metal, French, Swiss, Portuguese, Spanish and German—and that was all. There was nothing but money in the man's pockets.

Pat looked for suit labels and found none. She pointed out that it was obviously a tailor-made suit, and there should have been labels. She did not sound discouraged.

Monk fanned through the man's roll of money admiringly. "He sure goes well-heeled. Who do you suppose he is?"

Pat looked at Doc Savage. "What I'm wondering is why we grabbed him. Doc, don't you think you'd better tell us what this is all about?"

Doc told their driver in Portuguese, "Drive out through the Alcantara Valley."

Pat continued to watch him. Finally she said, "Come on, Doc. Let's have some information."

He said, "Now isn't the best time for that," and glanced meaningly at the driver.

"Oh," Pat said, and subsided.

Later he asked Pat, "Mind loaning me your gun?"

"What gun?"

He told her patiently, "That portable howitzer you carry in your handbag. I want to borrow it to influence our friend here."

Pat got the piece of artillery out of her handbag. "I can do without your wise sayings about this gun, this once," she said.

Doc said nothing, but Monk and Ham laughed. Pat's gun was an old-fashioned single-action six-shooter of Jesse James and Wild Bill Hickock vintage. It weighed more than four pounds, which was as much as some hunting rifles. The blunderbuss was a family heirloom, and they had always wondered whether Pat could hit anything with it.

Their driver got a glimpse of the gun. He became alarmed, judging from the way his color changed from mahogany to slate.

Doc selected a side road at random, told the driver to take it, then in a stretch of woods which looked lonesome, had the cab stop.

"Ham, you stay with the driver so he won't desert us," Doc suggested.

He seized the red-headed man and carried him into the woods. The fellow was showing no signs of consciousness.

"I didn't think I hit him that hard," Pat said uneasily. "His skull isn't cracked, or anything, is it?"

"He will wake up eventually," he told her.

This was not exactly true. The red-headed man was already awake. He had been conscious for about fifteen minutes, but doing a good job of pretending he wasn't.

Doc lowered the red-headed man beside some bushes, indicated Monk and Pat should watch the fellow, and said, "I'll look around to be sure we won't be bothered here."

He walked a few yards into the brush, and unloaded Pat's overgrown gun, putting the shells in his pocket. Then he went back.

"Coast seems clear." He made a pretense of taking the red-headed man's pulse.

"You're sure he's going to be all right?" Pat demanded.

Doc nodded.

"I'd better tell you something before we start questioning him," he said. "Listen to me, because there may not be time to repeat."

He hesitated, dangling Pat's six-shooter thoughtfully. He wanted to tell them some of the truth, enough truth to serve a purpose. But not too much. It was difficult to know what to say and what not to say.

He said, "This is no time for too many details. But here is the situation roughly: We have been handed a job, the job of finding a man. It would be more correct to say that our job is to catch a man. And don't get the idea that the matter isn't important because we have only one man to catch."

He paused, considering how best to convince them with words—and still not give specific facts—that they were involved in something extraordinary. It was a little like trying to describe the Grand Canyon to someone who had never heard of the place.

He hesitated to tell them in plain words how big it was, knowing he would sound over-dramatic, so spectacular that it would be incredible. It would sound too wild to say that the immediate course of the war, the lives of innumerable men, the future of European nations, depended on whether they caught one man. That was goofy stuff, if you put it in words. But it was not an exaggeration.

He said quietly, "If I told you how important it is that this one man be caught, it wouldn't be quite believable, I am afraid."

"Who wants us to catch the guy?" Monk demanded.

"The request came directly from the White House, which sounds rather wild also," he said, uncomfortably.

He crouched beside the red-headed man, still dangling Pat's six-gun idly in his fingers.

He added, "Here is what I'm trying to tell you: No one seems to know the whereabouts of this man we are to catch. However, I have a means of locating him which should work—and will work, providing no one interferes with us. Everything hinges on that— no one interfering with us. For that reason, we have to get tough with this fellow here. I do not know who he is, or what his game was, but he's out of

III

as nice but not spectacular. It was
do Paco, the spacious square, facing
uilding itself did not face the river,
of the sides, the side opposite the
me of the ministries.

ded entrance there was a wine shop

t wine," Doc told one of the two
s. "The brand I prefer is L'Impera-

tage?" the clerk asked.
eight."

e to visit our cellars and make a

one so naturally that Pat wasn't
s passing. She nudged Monk and
, and Monk said damned if he

a flight of steps into a typical
ool and spicy. The clerk showed
ttles, and the bottles had spots
aint on each. Doc selected a
bination, said, "I like this one.
re than you seem to have in

consult the wholesaler person-
pologetically. "I am sorry, but
t misunderstanding with the

20

luck. We can't have him interfering now. Because if things work out right, we'll be able to lay our hands right on this man we're supposed to catch."

He closed his eyes and thought: God help me, that is close to lying. He had never lied to Monk or Pat or Ham. Not exactly. He had shaved the truth a few times, and always regretted it.

While he was repenting, the red-headed man snatched the big six-shooter out of his hands.

The red-headed man was quick and violent. He was coming to his feet when he said, "Don't move, babies, or I'll blow you apart!"

The fellow stood there, as if afraid to make another move. He held the big gun too tightly, and it shook a little, enough to worry Monk and Pat—and it would have worried Doc if he hadn't unloaded it a while ago.

Pat stared at the gun. It was large, so much larger when you were looking at the producing end. Age and use had made the metal shiny and smooth, and the large ivory grips were as smooth as pearls from much use. The red-headed man's hand looked so strained that it was a little yellow on the grips, and it was sweating. Leaving a beautiful set of fingerprints, Pat thought. She hoped she wouldn't be shot with her own gun, not with a weapon that was a cherished heirloom like this one.

The red-headed man began backing away.

Doc said, "There are no shells in that gun."

The man laughed, but not as if it was funny. "You should know," he said.

"That's right, I should know," Doc said, and went toward him.

The red-headed man's face suddenly blanched. He pointed the gun at the ground. He pulled the trigger. Nothing happened except the hammer-fall click.

Monk said, "Damn, it's *not* loaded!" and he made for the man.

Doc Savage, to stop Monk, pretended to stumble and got under Monk's feet, bringing Monk down. They tied up in a pile in the grass.

The red-headed man threw the six-shooter at Doc. He threw it as hard as he could, missed Doc with the gun because Doc dodged, then whirled and tucked his elbows into his ribs and took out through the woods like a deer.

Pat said something wild and angry and chased the fellow. Pat was fast on her feet for a girl, but no equal of the red-headed man. He outdistanced her.

Doc told Monk in a low voice, "Don't catch him. Work at it, but don't catch him!"

Monk was dumfounded. "I'll be danged! You deliberately let him get away!"

Doc said, "Chase him. Make him think it's real."

They did that. They charged around through the thick woodland, carefully finding no trace of the red-headed man.

Doc said, "I'm going back and get Pat's gun. We've got to keep that cannon away from her, or she's going to shoot somebody."

Monk and Doc both searched for Pat's six-shooter in the brush, and found it before Pat joined them. Doc put the big weapon inside his shirt.

"We'll just forget to tell Pat we picked this up," he told Monk. "The way she likes to wave the thing around makes me nervous."

"Yeah, she has Buffalo Bill tendencies when she gets excited," Monk said.

Pat came back, and began hunting for her heirloom. Doc and Monk pretended to help for a few minutes.

Then Doc said, "We'll have to let it go."

"But that gun was Dad's!" Pat wailed. "I wouldn't take a fortune for it."

"We can't kill more time," Doc said.

Pat got mad.

"Look, you!" Pat poked Doc's chest angrily with a forefinger. "Next time you rig a piece of funny busi-

fellow, and he will not supply us more. I will give you his address, if you wish."

"I would appreciate that," Doc assured him.

The clerk wrote an address. "I would suggest that you not mention our firm, because it might irritate the distributor."

"Thank you. I won't."

When they were out on the street, Pat said, "Doc, was that a code deal, or not?"

"It was," he told her. He consulted the address the clerk had given him. "The spot seems to be north of Black Horse Square."

It wasn't too far, because Black Horse Square was the name the British used for the Praca do Commercio, which was also the Terreiro do Paco. They passed the triumphal arch on the north side, moved along Rua Augusta, and turned into an office building.

There they bought some more wine—bottles paint-marked blue and yellow—from a slick-haired, insulting young man.

"This is getting monotonous," Pat complained.

"You will pay upstairs," said the insulting young man.

The man they went to pay proved to be a red-faced, worried looking man who seized Doc Savage's hand, pumped it, and said, "I say, we're glad to see you, Savage. We've been in a bit of a wind lest you not make it."

Pat nudged Ham, said, "Hey, I've seen red-face before somewhere."

Ham said, "Good God!" in a low, impressed voice. Pat stared at him in surprise, because Ham was not easily impressed. She wondered who the dickens the red-faced man could be, but they were introduced before she could ask Ham. The red-faced man was presented as Mr. Dilling, but Pat didn't feel that his name was Mr. Dilling.

"Who is he?" Pat whispered, nudging Ham, after the introductions.

Ham told her. He told her as if he wasn't quite ready to believe a man so important would be out of England, or at least in Portugal, which was a neutral country and infested with foreign agents, hence somewhat dangerous.

"Hold your hat!" Ham whispered. "I don't think Doc was fooling when he said this thing was out of the ordinary."

Pat was plagued by a feeling of unreality. The red-faced man was no less an individual than the head of combined Allied intelligence.

They were taken into a comfortable room where there were some other men waiting. There was some hand-shaking, but it was without much feeling, as if no one was in a mood to waste time being social, or polite.

Mr. Dilling—which wasn't his name—got down to business by saying, "As I understand it, Mr. Savage, you prefer to work alone in this matter?"

"Not alone," Doc corrected him. "With my associates, here." He nodded at Monk, Ham and Pat.

"Are you planning for us to suspend efforts while you tackle the matter?"

"Not at all. That is just what I don't want. I put out no claim of being infallible. Suppose you fellows laid off, and we flopped?"

Mr. Dilling looked relieved. "That's sensible."

"I hope you can give me some information," Doc told him. "All I know about the situation is what you cabled me, and that was pretty general stuff."

Mr. Dilling nodded. He indicated one of the other men and said, "This is Festus, of Munich, and this is Melless, our Paris man."

Doc Savage listened to Mr. Dilling name the men who were present, and all of their names were familiar, and of some of them he had heard a great deal. It gave him a feeling of smallness, of inadequacy, to be in a room with so many men who were so capable along a special line.

He watched them, particularly those of whom he had heard special things. There was Oland Von Zett, for instance, who had assassinated the German General-in-Chief, Neufsedt, early in the war. Assassination was not the word the English and American general staff had used, but Zett with enormous cunning and patience had put six bullets through General Neufsedt and gotten away with it. General Neufsedt had started ordering the execution of American prisoners of war, and his assassination had put a stop to that.

There was also Francis Gonnerman, who had maneuvered the Italian coup, which had resulted in the surrender of the Italian government, the Italian fleet, and the flight of Mussolini. That had been a nice job. Gonnerman had not appeared in the newspapers in connection with the affair, because it was Gonnerman's business not to appear in any newspapers at all.

They didn't look like the hard, scheming, unbelievably adept fellows they really were, Doc Savage reflected. Von Zett didn't look old, nor did Gonnerman. Neither seemed as tough, even, as a regular soldier. They weren't suave slickers, either. They were just nice, healthy looking guys with whom you'd like to have a poker game or a round of golf. Which proved that you shouldn't look at a package and be too sure of what was inside it.

Mr. Dilling—who was a more remarkable fellow than any of the others, Doc knew—finished the introductions.

"Here is the situation," Mr. Dilling said.

Doc Savage listened, and his stomach wanted to crawl. Mr. Dilling didn't make a long speech. He tied a great deal up in a small matter-of-fact package of words and delivered it.

The war was near its end in Europe, and one of the Axis leaders was fleeing his nation. The man who was taking flight happened to be the only leader remaining with any great power. He was one of the most villainous of the lot. The man must be caught and punished.

"This information," Mr. Dilling explained, "came to us through various sources, and is absolutely true. We are sure of the facts."

Mr. Dilling took a large dossier of papers out of a briefcase. "Here are the reports," he said, "to substantiate what I have just told you. And there are other reports to substantiate what I am going to tell you next."

He seemed to deviate, because he began to talk about the state of the war. He sounded, for a moment, like a lecturer who had gotten his material from the newspapers; then he began to give facts and figures and names.

Germany was coming apart at the seams. The Nazis had been pounded until, like a great concrete block beaten with sledges, it had cracked in innumerable places.

"Their leader, as everybody knows, is a fanatic," Mr. Dilling said. "Whether or not he is crazy is a question. But one thing is sure—he is perfectly willing for every last German to die for Nazi plans."

Mr. Dilling scowled at his dossier of papers.

"The man has put a double in his place," he said. "He has disappeared, and left the double. Over a period of years, before the war even began, there was talk of the man using doubles to take his place. There was some truth in the talk. He had, however, only one double, a former shoe merchant named Ludorff, from Minden, who resembles him closely in appearance and voice."

"The double is going to be assassinated, so that the Nazi chief will appear to have died a martyr. You men know the German temperament, so you know what will happen if the man appears to die a martyr. Germany will become solid again. The cracks in that shattering concrete block will be cemented together. The cement tying it together will be the supposed martyrdom of the Nazi leader.

"The assassination of their leader, and the job is to be done so that it will appear to be the work of Allied agents, will prolong the war. As to how many lives that will cost, your guess is as good as mine. Thousands, at least.

"And there is another hellish probability: Nazism will be glorified in the minds of the German people, by the death of the leader. It will live. And in time—twenty years, people are always saying—we will have this mess again."

Mr. Dilling had finished. He said, "All right. Questions."

"What ideas," Doc asked, "have you about where he might be?"

"Not a damned one."

"Eh?"

"The fellow has disappeared absolutely. We can't give you the least idea of where he is."

One of the other men—it was Francis Gonnerman, of the Italian coup—said gravely, "The thing has us gray-headed. The basic problem is simple: Catch this fellow and show the German people the ratty trick he was pulling in skipping out and leaving a double to be murdered in his place."

Doc asked, "How much time have we?"

"Before they assassinate the double? Two days. We are sure that we have two days. And I'm telling you, that isn't much time."

"As soon as we catch the real leader, and broadcast the fact, they won't assassinate the double."

"No. There would be no point."

Doc Savage frowned. "The man has changed his appearance, probably."

"No doubt."

"Have you his fingerprints?"

Gonnerman smiled grimly. "We have the only set in existence, as far as we know. They were taken by a police sergeant named Moestez in Munich following the well-known beer hall putsch. Later, after the Nazis came into power, he had all his police records destroyed, with particular attention to fingerprints. But Moestez kept these prints as a souvenir, and we have them."

"You are certain they are genuine?"

"Quite." Gonnerman indicated the dossier which Mr. Dilling was holding. "You will find a copy in there."

Doc Savage nodded. He had, now that he had heard the assignment, a heavier feeling than before about the thing. The fear was still with him, the same fear that had started to plague him on the flight across the Atlantic, when he'd had too much time to think. Out of this talk he had gotten a definite, bitter feeling of hopelessness.

Two days, he thought. Two days wasn't much time, and the immensity of the job was terrifying. He wished, with sharp aching violence, that the infernally crazy world would finally come to its senses and things like this would no longer be happening.

It was a mad, wild thing that one fanatic ex-paperhanger could cause so much terror and suffering, and this present thing of taking flight and leaving a double to be murdered and martyred was as wild as anything before.

Thinking how hair-brained it is doesn't help, he reflected wryly.

He looked up, and began to describe the red-headed man. He gave a complete word picture of the man, then asked, "Know him, any of you?"

"His name, I think, is Hans Berkshire. No record."

"He got on my trail," Doc said. "I thought he might be a Nazi agent assigned to the job of finding out just why I was in Lisbon. So I caught him, let him find out I was here to catch a man, and turned him loose."

Mr. Dilling didn't like that. "I don't understand why you would do such a thing!"

"It was an idea."

Dilling frowned. "I don't get it."

Doc leaned forward. "We have no idea where our

man is to be found. We might waste months hunting him."

"Yes, but—"

"My idea is to draw attention to myself, disclose that I am after the Nazi leader. That was my purpose in handling the red-headed man as—"

"My God, you'll pull them down on your head!" Dilling said violently. "They'll try to wipe you out! The minute they learn that you are on the job, they'll drop everything and try to get rid of you. And don't think they won't! Don't underestimate the effect you'll have on those fellows, Mr. Savage."

Doc said, "The attack on me will perhaps be made by someone in the confidence of the Nazi leader."

"Of course it will. They wouldn't take a chance of bringing in an outsider on a thing like this. The Nazi chief just took a few choice scamps into his confidence in this thing. We know that."

"Then whoever jumps me will probably know where the Fuehrer is."

"Yes, but—" Mr. Dilling squinted thoughtfully at Savage. "Well, now—I think I begin to get your thought."

"It might work."

"If it does, it'll definitely be a short-cut," Dilling said. He began to show some enthusiasm. "You might get on their trail immediately. You might, at that."

"I hope so."

"Can we help you?"

"When I get something definite in the way of information," Doc told him, "you'll know it immediately, if possible. I have no intention of trying to wade through a thing as big as this single-handed."

Mr. Dilling looked relieved. "I was worried about that," he said. "I had heard that you preferred to work alone."

"Only when it seems better," Doc said. "Where can I go over the reports in your dossier?"

"There is a private room in the back."

Doc Savage made a rather queer request before

he parted from Monk, Ham and Pat. "Pat," he said, "would you do me a favor?"

"Eh?"

"Loan me your six-shooter."

"You could get hold of a lot better shooting iron," Pat said. "After all, this was made before the day of Jesse James."

"But would you loan it to me?"

"Sure," Pat said.

She was puzzled. Since Doc had made an issue of having the gun, she had a suspicion it had somehow become important.

IV

Monk and Ham and Pat had a conference. They held it in the back of the room, where they were by themselves, and Ham began it by remarking that he was impressed by the kind of men who were here. "The more you think about it, the more it begins to stand your hair on end," he said.

Pat leaned forward and whispered nervously, "I'm not enthusiastic about this."

Monk was surprised. "What's the matter with you, Pat? There'll be some hell-tearing excitement before this is over with, and that's what you were interested in."

Pat shook her head. "I didn't mean that."

"No?"

"Listen, the Nazis and everyone else has known for months that Germany is licked. So this scheme probably wasn't hatched up on the spur of the moment."

Ham said, "You have something, I would say. Take the matter of the fingerprints. He had all his fingerprints collected years ago, which would indicate something like this has been in the back of his mind a long time."

Pat nodded. "All right, the thing is well prepared. That's a safe bet. Therefore they've got a tight, vicious little group which is prepared to do anything to put this over."

Ham began to get the drift of Pat's thinking. He said, "More than that, they can call on the whole

German secret police service, the Gestapo and everything else, in an emergency."

"That's right."

Monk muttered gloomily, "Doc surely knows what
he's doing. He thought of all that before he decided
to pull them down on his head."

"That's right," Pat agreed. "But he should have
consulted us about it."

"I don't see why—"

"Look, fellows, I don't know how it hits you, but
it strikes me that Doc shouldn't be taking that risk
himself."

Ham admitted, "That worried me."

"Yes, and me, too. Let's not kid ourselves. Ham,
you and Monk both are pretty good when you get
mixed up in trouble, but I'm not trying to belittle
you when I say that you're not as good as Doc."

Ham said, "Don't worry about hurting our feelings
on that score." He gestured at the men who had
been present at the meeting. "Do you think guys of
that calibre would turn out in force to confer with
us? Fat chance. They're here to meet Doc Savage.
If you noticed carefully, you could see that every
one of them was in awe of Doc."

Pouncing on that point, Pat said, "If Doc takes
this risk of drawing an attack on himself, and loses,
they'll kill him. And that would mean more than
Doc losing his life. It would mean the Nazi leader
will probably get away with this final, dirty trick."

Ham frowned. "What're you getting at?"

"Suppose we serve as the bait, not Doc," Pat said
grimly.

It took five minutes of sober-faced mumbling for
them to decide to follow Pat's suggestion. The telling
would have to be done later, because Doc was sure
to veto the idea now. They would have to tell Doc,
of course, and preferably before the Nazi group
pounced on the "bait."

"When will we do this?" Monk asked.

"What's the matter with right now?" Pat demanded.

They went into the inner room, looking innocent, where Doc Savage was seated at a desk going through Mr. Dilling's dossier on the case.

"Anything we can do to help?" Ham asked.

Doc shook his head. "There seems to be a great deal of detail here, but it doesn't add anything to the basic fact that the Nazi chief has disappeared and left a double in his place, and the double is to be murdered in order to solidify the spirit of the Germans."

Doc separated several sheets from the dossier.

"However, you will want to go over these," he added. "Here are descriptions of the Nazi agents involved intimately in the plot with the Fuehrer. You will want to memorize the data. You'll find photographs and fingerprints. I suggest you get off by yourselves and hold a memorizing session."

Monk took the identification sheets, asked, "Any objections to our going back to the hotel to study these?"

"Better not," Doc said. "If that red-headed fellow passes the word around, they will be watching the hotel."

Pat said, "We'll go somewhere. We'll call you in an hour or so."

"All right."

They left the building, Monk with the identification sheets in his pocket. They found a cab.

Pat told the cab driver, "The Hotel Chiaro di Luna."

"Hey, Doc said not to go there," Monk exclaimed.

"We didn't say we wouldn't," Pat reminded him.

Monk hesitated, finally grinned without much genuine glee, and sank back on the cushions. "I guess if we're to take over that bait job ourselves, now is as good a time as any," he said.

Ham frowned, not pleased and not approving. He had gone against Doc's wishes before, and usually he landed in trouble. He scowled at Monk. Monk was a precipitous fellow who liked to tear directly into an obstacle, preferably without any preliminary beating together of brains.

Toward the end of the ride to the hotel, Ham got a wry expression, for it dawned on him that Pat had sucked them into one of her wild schemes. The whole idea of their being the bait, instead of Doc, was Pat's notion. She had hatched it, and she had sold it to them.

"Pat," Ham said.

"Yes?"

"I can see why Doc hated to have you turn up in this affair."

"Says which?"

"You're a doubtful influence. You're a shot of wild-juice. In other words, you just sold us a bill of goods."

"I sold you nothing!" Pat said cheerfully. "I just had a good idea, and you thought it was good, and so here we are."

"Such innocence," Ham muttered, "will no doubt get us all in a mess."

They alighted from the cab in front of the Hotel Chiaro di Luna, discovered the fare was ten escudos, and had a row with the pirate driver. None of them could speak Portuguese to any extent, and in the middle of the fuss they got some volunteer help. The volunteer was a lean, blond young-looking man who grinned at Pat and said, "I know some words for this fellow."

His words made the hack driver decide that one escudo, which was about one dollar American, was nearer the correct fee.

"Thanks," Pat said.

"My name is Carter," the blond young man said.

"Well, thank you again," Pat told him.

The young man didn't take leave of them. Instead, he accompanied them into the hotel, crowded into the small antique elevator with them, and got out on the same floor. He was following them.

Monk lost his patience. "Look, blondy, what goes

on?" he demanded. "You forming an attachment, or something?"

The blond young man grinned. "I wanted to talk to you about Berkshire."

"Eh?"

"Berkshire. Not very tall, red-headed, some freckles, weight about one sixty, big grin and a fund of corny jokes. Hans Berkshire."

"Oh!" Monk said.

"Mr. Carter," Pat said, "you are perfectly welcome to trail right along with us, but keep making words."

Carter smiled, examined Pat again and said, "You are lovely, if I may insert such a statement at this point."

Monk had been examining Mr. Carter doubtfully, and finally came to the conclusion that he didn't think a lot of the guy.

"So your name is Carter," Monk said. "Carter what?"

"Just Carter," Carter told him. "My name actually isn't Carter, so Carter will do as good as any for a designation. A name is but a handle on a man, as the Romans say."

They reached the ornate, slightly sinful plush-lined suites of rooms which Monk and Ham had taken. Monk looked in the closets and behind things, found no one, turned and asked Carter, "Any microphones hidden around here?"

"Just one," Carter said.

"Where?"

Carter moved a chair under the light fixture which dangled from the ceiling, climbed on to it, and unscrewed one of the light bulbs from the fixture. He passed the bulb down, saying, "It isn't made of glass at all, you'll find, and the bulb serves as a diaphragm for the microphone. To install the thing, they had to rewire the lighting circuit. But the idea is rather clever. You'd think it was merely a burned out bulb. You would unscrew it and throw it away without noticing the difference, probably."

Monk scowled. "How come you knew it was there?"

"I'll get to that in a minute," the blond young man said. He got out a cigarette and a long amber holder and got the cigarette going. "I'm going to review the situation," he said. "To put it briefly, the Nazi leader has fled, leaving behind a double who is to be killed so that it will seem the leader died a martyr's death. The object in doing this is twofold. First, the martyred death of the Nazi chief will probably pull the German people together and make them fight a while longer —"

"Will it?" Monk interrupted. "Haven't they got more sense?"

"It'll pull the Germans together the way Pearl Harbor united the Americans," Carter said.

"You seem pretty sure."

"I should be. I'm a German."

"You don't look it!" Monk said suspiciously.

"*Es steht bei Ihnen*," Carter told him. "*Warum nicht?* All upper-class Europeans, as a matter of fact, look pretty much alike. I am German, all right. I was lecturer in psychology, specializing in isolates, at the new university in Dresden."

Monk scowled. "Brother, you don't even have a Fritz accent."

"I hope not. I went to Oxford, old fellow, and if they don't take an accent out of you at Oxford, it can't be done. Just take it from me, my boy. I'm a genuine German, one of the educated, intelligent ones —if you are willing to admit there could be such a German."

Monk wasn't convinced, but he could see nothing to hang an argument on. "What gives you a claim to being intelligent, you figure?"

Carter leaned forward. "If the Fuehrer gets away with this trick—if he makes the German people believe he died a martyr—the whole creed of Nazism, of National Socialism and all that goes with it, will live. You may defeat it now, but it will live. It will become a faith, something like religion, something you can't stamp out."

Carter paused to stare at them. He looked grim, hard-lipped, emphatic.

"I wouldn't like that," he said. "I belong to a group who wouldn't like it. I and the men associated with me are trying to stop it, because we don't want Germany to be re-born after this war with Nazism in its soul." Some of the violence left him, and he looked at them again. "On that I base my claim for being an intelligent German."

"That shuts me up," Monk admitted. "What about this red-headed Berkshire?"

Carter smiled slightly and said, "It would be better if you would let me talk to him."

"Huh?"

"Talk to Berkshire, the red-headed man," Carter said patiently.

"Just what," Monk asked, "gives you the idea we would do that?"

"Didn't you capture him?"

"When was that?"

"I wish you didn't feel you had to be so innocent with me," Carter said. "As a matter of fact, we know that Miss Patricia Savage black-jacked Berkshire in the park a couple of blocks from here. Then you carried him off in a cab. So I presume you have him safe."

"So you knew that!"

Carter laughed, and the mirth sounded hearty and genuine. "I imagine Berkshire has told you quite a remarkable story, hasn't he?"

"How do you mean?"

Carter lost his mirthful expression, and finally frowned. "Look here, why are you beating around the bush?"

"Brother, you're a great one to accuse us of bush-beating," Monk told him violently. "You've been talking a blue streak since you came up here, and the total of what you've said is practically nothing. Now what do you want, anyway?"

"I want Berkshire!" Carter said bluntly.

"Why?"

"Because I want him. Is that reason enough?"

"Tough, eh?" Monk said.

The blond man took a hand out of his hat—he had been holding the hat in his hands—and the hat contained a shiny gun. "Or would you prefer a reason of this sort?" he demanded.

Monk stared at the gun, and he had a queer feeling in the region back of his second vest button, not because he was afraid of guns, but because he saw they had been taken in. He didn't fear guns, but he respected them. This one was a Walther Model PP, known as the presentation model because of the flossy engraving, gold plating and ivory grips. It wasn't a bad gun. German made.

Monk indicated the weapon—careful to make no sudden moves—and asked, "You in earnest with that thing?"

"I would regret killing all three of you," Carter said in a flat meaningful way. "But I would do it."

Pat said, "Monk, he means it."

Monk wasn't sure. He didn't care to find out. He said, "At finding Berkshire you are out of luck. We had him. He's gone. He got away."

"*Wie schade!*" Carter said, and Monk was suddenly sure the young man was German. He hadn't been certain of it before. But now Carter's speech had taken on a guttural quality that was completely Teutonic.

"Mr. Carter," Pat said.

"*Ja, fräulein?*"

"If you are a German patriot working against the Fuehrer, who does that make Mr. Berkshire?" Pat asked.

Carter smiled thinly, thoughtfully. "You really do not know who this Berkshire is?"

"Should we?"

"You are much less efficient than your reputations claim you to be if you don't know who he is."

Pat said, "Oh, nuts! Talk, talk, and it gets us nowhere."

"You want action?"

"It would be a change."

Carter moved his gun menacingly. "All right. We'll have some action. Your hands up, please. I am going to search you."

He went over them, one at a time, with quick efficiency. He discovered that Monk and Ham were wearing bulletproof vests, and made them remove these.

He said, "Get over there in the corner." When they were in the corner, he demanded of Pat, "Where is that gun of yours?"

"What gun?"

"That howitzer I hear you pack," Carter said. "I want it."

"Why?"

He stared at Pat, and Pat suddenly had an unnerving feeling that the man wanted her gun more than he wanted anything.

"I haven't got it," Pat said.

He stared at her a while longer.

"That's good," he said. "I wouldn't want to be shot with such a thing as I hear it is." But he didn't sound satisfied, or pleased.

He went to the window.

He took a yellow handkerchief out of his pocket, tucked it in the pullcord of the window shade, and let it hang there, where it could be seen from the side street which the window faced.

"It will take my friends a few minutes to get here," he remarked.

Monk and the others said nothing.

"I wish you knew where Berkshire is," Carter said gloomily. "We want that fellow very badly indeed."

"Wish we could help you," Pat said dryly.

Carter stared at her.

"By the way," he said, "where is your old-fashioned, western six-shooter? I want that, too."

"I haven't got it," Pat said.

Carter developed a strange sick look.

V

Carter's friends were half a dozen blocky gentlemen who looked as if they were without souls. They knocked on the door, then came in when Carter invited them, and each gave Carter a heel click and a poker-faced expression that could mean anything. They were, Monk reflected, as slab-faced a group as he had ever seen.

"The butcher's half-dozen," Pat whispered.

"Somebody has been feeding them on crows, from their looks," Monk agreed.

Carter told the newcomers in German, "They say they do not know where Berkshire is. They may be lying. I do not think so, because I gave them a very good story about being a patriotic German who wanted to thwart the plan."

Monk said, "Speak English, dammit. We don't understand German."

Which was a lie, because they could at least understand German. And it didn't fool Carter.

"You have a slopping acquaintance with German and about twenty other languages, and you know it," Carter said.

Monk demanded, "Aren't you a German patriot?"

"Very," Carter said.

Monk didn't agree. "You're a damned liar!"

"I'm a damned liar," Carter said.

Carter then turned to the six newcomers again, and told them in German that Monk, Ham and Pat must be taken from the hotel without attracting

39

notice. If notice was attracted, Carter told them, they might as well make a good job of it and shoot Monk and Ham and Pat on the spot, and shoot anyone else whom they cared to. The blank-faced gentlemen soaked this in with hair-raising solemnity.

One of the blank-faces asked, in excellent English, "Why bother with them?"

"We don't intend to bother too much," Carter said, also in English. "I hope they understand that." He turned to the prisoners. "Do you?"

"You keep on, and you'll scare us," Monk muttered.

"You will link arms with three of my friends," Carter told them. "The other three friends and myself will accompany you."

"Your three friends look like zombies," Pat told him.

One of the zombies gave a cold-blooded laugh and gripped Pat's wrist. She suddenly discovered there was a handcuff around her wrist. She was fastened to the man.

She looked up at the man, and the fellow's expression gave her a fright. The feeling she got was sudden and so clammy that she tried instinctively to jerk away. She had the feeling, abruptly, of being close to something that was pretty awful. It was about the same sensation that contact with a corpse would give her.

Her face must have mirrored her feelings, because Ham Brooks said, "Grab the handlebars, Pat. Don't get to reeling."

"I wish I was back in New York," Pat said, then realized that what she had said, and her tone, sounded like a scared child. "I wonder why he wanted my six-shooter so bad?" she asked.

The blank-faced man jerked at her wrist, tugging her out into the corridor. She had, with growing intensity, a feeling of repellence, a sensation of being actually attached to a cadaver. She was suddenly convinced that the men would not hesitate to kill her.

The front entrance of the hotel consisted of two doors, one on each side of a center post. Both doors were open, and Pat noticed that part of the group ahead went out through one door and the rest through the other. Monk through the right side, and Ham through the left. It gave her an idea.

She pushed against her captor—with the feeling she was against a corpse—and persuaded him to go through the right-hand door. She was on his left, attached to his left wrist with about six inches of handcuff linkage.

At the last minute, Pat stepped left, went through the left side of the door, reached out and gave the open door a quick jerk shut.

She was on one side of the center post, her captor on the other, when the heavy door slapped shut, against the handcuff linkage.

Pat did a good job in acting startled. She gave a violent jump—which was designed to wedge the handcuff chain inextricably. It succeeded fairly well. The chain was thin, the door didn't fit too well, and Pat's yank put considerable force on the thing.

"We're caught!" Pat said innocently. "Get me loose!"

Carter came back to her and said malevolently, "You did that on purpose!" But he didn't sound as if he was sure.

At this point, the zombie on the other side of the door got panicky and gave the door a kick, trying to force it open. As a result, the door wedged solid.

Carter cursed the blank-faced man's stupidity.

Monk, out on the sidewalk, said loudly, "Look at the cops coming!"

"*Sonderbarerweise!*" Carter blurted, and jumped back to take a look down the street. "*Es ist!*"

He was German all right, Pat decided, because that was the language he went back to when he was excited.

The men coming down the street were not city

policemen. They were military shore patrol, arm-banded and on duty, which was worse.

Carter said, "Get them in the car!"

Monk and Ham were bustled into a long, swanky looking touring car which was parked at the curbing.

Carter gave the door a couple of angry kicks. On the other side, the zombie was fighting the wedged panel. Pat, figuring Carter was the most likely to get it open, managed to make a showing of helping—and get in Carter's way so he couldn't kick the door effectively.

Carter went around to the other side of the door.

"I am going to kick your brains out," he told the blank-faced man.

And he kicked the zombie in the pants. It was the first time Pat had ever seen a kick in the stern that didn't strike her as funny. There is something, comedians know, infallibly funny about a kick in the rear. But this one raised Pat's hair. If a kick could have killed the man, Carter would have done it. The kicked man made a hoarse damp-sounding croak of agony.

"I trust you have a happy time of it," Carter told the blank man.

Then Carter hurried to the car, got in and the car drove away.

Pat started to shriek an alarm. She changed her mind, convinced that if trouble started, Monk and Ham would be shot immediately.

The shore police came abreast.

"Do you speak English?" Pat asked, smiling.

"Yes, Miss," one of the soldiers said.

"I am a detective," Pat said, lying convincingly. "I was taking my prisoner out of the hotel, and he managed to get us jammed in this door. Will you help me?"

The soldiers grinned. They were delighted by such a pretty girl.

"We certainly will help," one assured Pat.

They began laboring with the wedged door. Two of them, by shoving, managed to get the door free.

Pat stared at the blank-faced man, wondering why he was taking this. He could understand English, she knew. But he was doing nothing but stand there and look like a crook, a part he was naturally equipped for.

He's got a gun, of course, Pat thought.

"Will you search him for me, please?" Pat asked one of the helpful soldiers. "I am just wondering if one of his friends could have slipped him a gun."

"Of a certainty," said a soldier gallantly.

He searched. Pat's eyes popped. The blank-faced man was unarmed. He didn't have a thing in the way of a weapon. He'd had a gun. How in the dickens, Pat pondered, did he make away with the weapon?

The mystery dumfounded her for a minute. Then she sank to a knee, made a pretense of adjusting her slipper tie, and raked the floor with her eyes.

"Excuse me," she said.

She went over to a divan and got the man's pistol from under the divan, where he had scooted it without her noticing. The gun was another Walther, this one black and ugly.

Pat came back blithely and said, "I tossed my gun away when we got hung up. I was afraid he would get it."

The military police laughed. They were all young men, and they thought she was cute. They said so. They told her she was too pretty to be a detective. Pat asked them to get her a taxicab. They did. One of them got her telephone number.

Pat waved at them as the cab drove off. She was pleased with herself. Her prisoner, the blank-faced man, was sitting sidewise on the seat to favor the place where Carter had kicked him.

Pat said, "It was a shame the way he kicked you. You should pay him back for that."

"In what way?"

"You could tell us where the Fuehrer is."

The man didn't change expression. "When we get kicked, we have it coming to us. Anyway, I can kick someone of less rank than myself."

"You pass those things along, eh?"

"That's right."

"Are you going to tell me where the Nazi chief is?"

"No."

"Want to bet you don't?" Pat asked.

She was going to take the man to Doc Savage. Doc would get information out of him. Doc was by profession a surgeon and physician, and he had a combination of lie detectors and truth serum which he used on fellows like this one, and it was almost infallible.

Pat hadn't noticed much about the driver, except that the driver was very young.

"Boy!" she called to the driver. "Take the Rue Augusta, and I will tell you when to turn."

The driver wasn't a boy. It was a girl, red-headed, and nice. She pulled over to the curb, stopped, and said, "I'm sorry, Miss, but I am not too familiar with the city yet. Would you show me on the map?"

Pat said, "Okay. Where's your map?" And the driver leaned back over the front seat with a map. Pat eyed the map, and was putting her finger on the Rue Augusta when the driver moved quickly. She snatched Pat's gun.

The red-headed girl got the gun and jerked back. She let Pat look at the business end of the thing. "You know whether it's loaded, or not."

Pat, dumfounded, had a silly moment and said, "I wouldn't know a thing about what's in the gun. Ask old dead-face, here."

The zombie said, "It is not loaded."

He said it with a flat matter-of-factness that was utterly convincing. And then—to Pat—the unexpected happened. The red-headed girl was taken in. She jacked the slide of the automatic back to look in the chamber.

The blank-faced man lunged, got hold of the gun.

"Watch him!" Pat shrieked. She was much more afraid of the man than of the girl. She dived for the gun herself.

For what seemed minutes, six hands fought for possession of the gun. The expressionless man struggled without words or excitement, coldly and viciously, and Pat got the sick feeling that he would begin shooting if he got the weapon.

Finally, to keep anyone from getting possession of the Walther, Pat began beating the cluster of hands against the edge of the window.

The gun flew out into the street.

The blank-faced man jerked away and piled out the other door of the cab. He ran for the nearest side street.

Pat scrambled out to get the gun. She scooped it up, worried with the safety a moment, and leveled the weapon. When she had what she hoped was a bead on the runner's legs, she fired.

The street became full of gun-thunder. The weapon was loaded, all right. It was full. Eight cartridges. Pat fired them all.

She apparently didn't scratch the zombie, and he popped into the side street.

Pat pointed the empty gun at the red-headed girl and screamed, "Chase him! Run him down with the car!"

The red-headed girl scrambled behind the wheel. The old car jumped violently—and stopped. The engine roared. Nothing happened.

"The gears are stripped!" the red-headed girl gasped.

Pat said, "Don't pull that on me!" She shoved the other girl over angrily, and tried the gears herself. Nothing happened. Something had broken.

Pat got out and ran to the side street. But the

blank-faced man was gone. The red-headed girl followed Pat, and Pat demanded, "Shall we follow him? Hunt for him, I mean."

"I didn't like his looks," the red-headed girl said.

"I didn't either," Pat admitted. "Let's get out of here."

When they had walked four blocks, each block in a different direction, the red-haired girl said, "My knees have got the shakes. Can't we stop somewhere?"

"It's a good idea," Pat agreed. "Here's a place." She indicated a sidewalk cafe which seemed placid enough. They got a table behind a cluster of phony-looking potted bushes, and sank into chairs.

"Whew!" Pat exclaimed. "Things got to going too fast for me."

The red-headed girl said, "I'm Barni Cuadrado. You do not know me, of course."

A waiter came. Pat ordered coffee and hot milk, half and half, stumbling with the Portuguese words, until the other girl helped her out. The waiter went away.

"All right, Barni," Pat said grimly. "Who the dickens are you? And what were you trying to do?"

Barni Cuadrado asked, "Aren't you Patricia Savage?"

"Yes."

"Then I bungled what I was trying to do."

"Which was what?"

The red-headed girl hesitated, frowning. "It's so simple to explain, but I don't know exactly how to start. Suppose I begin this way: Something very big is happening, something so important that whole nations and even the war itself are involved." She bogged down, looking dissatisfied with her words.

"That's too general, isn't it?" she continued. "The truth is this: The Fuehrer is fleeing Germany. He has left a double behind, who is to be murdered so that the Fuehrer will appear to have died a hero. You have to know the German people to realize how horrible the plan is, how it will unite them and prolong a hopeless war, how it will glorify the Nazi National Socialist ideology in the minds of the German people until they will never forget it. In other words, how it will be the seed for another war in the future."

"That's amazing!" Pat exclaimed, pretending she hadn't known a thing about it.

Barni Cuadrado nodded. "It is terrible. But there's at least one organized group of Germans who know it. And they are out to thwart the plan, to stop it."

She looked at Pat steadily.

"My cousin, Hans Berkshire, is head of the group trying to stop the thing," she said. "I am helping him."

Pat hoped she didn't look as amazed as she felt. She said nothing.

Barni continued, "Berkshire heard that the Allied intelligence had heard of the Fuehrer's plan, and that they had called in Doc Savage to stop the thing. Berkshire wishes to work with Mr. Savage."

"Holy smoke!" Pat said softly. Doc, she thought, had made a bum guess. Doc had thought the red-headed Berkshire was one of the Fuehrer's men.

"Things have gotten into a mess," Barni said. "Berkshire knew somehow that Mr. Savage was coming by plane, so he watched all the planes, and he saw a man he thought was Mr. Savage. He tried to trail Mr. Savage, but Mr. Savage laid some kind of trap, and grabbed Berkshire. The unfortunate part of this was that Berkshire wasn't actually sure the man was Mr. Savage—the thing that got him to doubting was the way the man he supposed was Mr. Savage gave away the fact that he was in Europe to find the German leader. Berkshire didn't think Mr. Savage would be so careless. Anyway, Berkshire escaped."

"Where is he now?" Pat demanded.

"Hiding," Barni explained. "He sent me to the hotel

where you had been staying. My job was to get you and find out if Doc Savage was really in Portugal."

"That's why you were so handy outside the hotel then?"

"Yes. I was pretending to be a taxi driver. It was just luck that the soldiers called me to pick up you and that fellow."

"Did you know that sober-faced fellow?"

"No."

"Was he one of the Nazi outfit?"

"I don't know. He could be."

Pat frowned. "Does this Berkshire know anything that would help Doc Savage?"

"He thinks he does." Barni nodded earnestly. "I should think he would. He has an amazing fund of inside knowledge."

"Let's get him," Pat said, "and take him to Doc."

Barni stood up eagerly. "That's exactly what he wants."

VI

A waiter came to them. He looked upset, almost sick. He said in Portuguese, "You must go, immediately."

Pat didn't understand him, and asked him what he'd said. The waiter twisted his napkin in his hands, got as red as a firecracker, and began to pop like one when he spoke. Pat couldn't get Portuguese spoken so fast. But she saw Barni show shock.

"What is it?" Pat demanded.

"He was offered a thousand marks, German, to put something in our coffee," Barni explained.

"Let's get out of here," Pat said quickly.

They paid the check, and Pat gave the waiter some money, not quite a thousand marks, but all she could afford, for his trouble. She wanted his address so she could pay him more, but he wouldn't give it to her.

Barni gripped Pat's arm uneasily. "I'm scared all over again," she said. "They must have found out where we were. Do—do you suppose it was poison he asked the waiter to put in our coffee?"

"What else could it have been?" Pat was nervous herself. She walked rapidly.

She wasn't much inclined to remember statistical facts, but one popped into her thoughts: Fear, the dictionary says, is the painful emotion characteristic of the apprehension of evil. That's what I've got, Pat reflected.

49

"Barni, we even forgot to ask the waiter what the man looked like."

Barni nodded. "All I could think of was getting out of there."

"We've got to get Berkshire, then find Doc Savage," Pat said. "And quick. How long will it take us to find Berkshire?"

"An hour, probably."

"Oh Lord, that's too long!" Pat gasped. "We'll go to Doc first. I've got to tell him that Monk and Ham are in trouble."

"Where is he?"

That, Pat thought, is a slight problem. She had seen enough of the Allied Intelligence Headquarters north of Black Horse Square to know that it was very hush-hush. A man as important as Mr. Dilling, who was in charge of the Allied side of the affair, couldn't afford to draw public attention. She could imagine Mr. Dilling's exasperation if she walked in with a strange girl she had picked up, even if the girl did have an interesting story.

"We'll find Doc," Pat said, and began to wonder how.

They walked north, then turned west. It was late afternoon, past the lazy siesta hour, but not early enough for the promenade crowds. The sidewalks were moderately crowded.

Barni glanced behind frequently, and finally she said, "Pat, I think we're being followed."

Pat discovered that her mouth had gone suddenly dry. She had to swallow before she could say, "What does he look like? And where is he?"

"A man in a black suit," Barni said. "He's on the other side of the street."

Pat had to swallow again before she could say, "All right, let's stop and admire this window, and I'll take a look."

She had no trouble locating the shadow. Black suits were not plentiful on Lisbon streets at this hour.

She saw the man, and her flesh seemed to crawl on her bones.

"It's one of the dead-faced men!" she gasped.

Fear came into their hearts then. Pat, who didn't scare easily, was not proud of the way she began feeling. Fear had never bothered her much. She had even boasted a few times that she enjoyed the sensation, that it was a thrill of a certain sort, something that she looked back on with appreciation. She wouldn't look back on the way she felt now. Never. The feeling was like worms.

It was the blank-faced man, of course. Not just that one in the black suit following them. There was another. She saw him a moment later, looking out of a passing car.

"They're all around us!" she told Barni, and her voice had a wooden coffin sound to her ears.

They walked rapidly, and Barni said, "I hope we find a policeman." But they did not find a policeman. There was not a uniform in sight.

Pat said, "Let's stay on the main streets. I think this one has more of a crowd."

She started to turn. Then Barni screamed, snatched at Pat's arms and jerked her back. As dark and silent as death coming in sleep, a black limousine slipped through the spot Pat would have occupied if Barni hadn't stopped her.

Pat shrank back. She was certain her face had the color of a peeled banana. She was certain there was another of the zombies in the car.

"They're trying to kill us," Barni said.

Pat said, "Come on!"

"What are you going to do?"

"Run. At least that will confuse them. And it's what I feel like doing."

So they ran. They got in the middle of the sidewalk, glued their elbows to their sides, and ran. It had no dignity, but it covered ground.

Running built up their fright. Pat felt panic growing, but didn't know why. Then she knew that the running was feeding the fright, but she didn't have the nerve to stop.

Suddenly Pat wheeled around, making a U-turn, not slackening speed.

"In here!" she gasped. "What luck!"

She had discovered they were on the Terreiro do Paco, and passing the wine shop where Doc had gone to get his directions to the meeting with Mr. Dilling and his group.

The same two middle-aged clerks were on duty. They gaped at Pat.

"They're trying to kill us!" Pat gasped. "Watch the door!"

The mild-looking old clerks acted confused.

"Senhorita, it is the police you should see," one told her.

Pat was in no mood for innocence. One of the middle-aged men wore a regimental necktie, somewhat on the gaudy side. Pat got hold of the tie suddenly, jerked the gentleman forward across the counter.

"You get hold of Doc Savage—and quick!" she said grimly. "Tell him Pat is in a mess, and scared stiff."

The old fellow looked at her.

"Go into the back room," he said. "And wait."

The back room proved to be an office, ancient and genteel and subdued. Just like the libraries in the detective stories where they find the bodies, Pat thought. One of the elderly clerks closed the door on them. Pat went over to the door quickly. It was locked.

"Are they all right?" Barni asked nervously.

"I think so," Pat said, then added uneasily, "On second thought, I don't know."

"What will we do?"

"Wait, I guess."

Barni nodded. She looked frightened. After a few minutes, as if to fight the silence in the room, she began talking. "I am not used to this sort of thing," she said. "I am Swiss. In Switzerland, your folks do not bring you up for such things as this."

"I've been to Switzerland," Pat said. "I liked it."

Barni nodded. "I was born in Interlaken, which is a little town that all the tourists know. My father was a wood-carver, or rather he had a shop employing several wood-carvers who made those little gimcracks the tourists buy. It was a very pleasant existence, but I didn't like it. Interlaken is a little town, and I resented it, the way so many girls resent the small towns in which they grow up." She looked at Pat wryly. "I wish I was back there."

"Have you been away long?" Pat asked.

"Oh, no. I'm not an adventuress. Don't get that idea. I have been in Paris and Rome, but that was when I was a young girl, before the war began. Actually, this is the first time I've been out of Switzerland in nearly five years."

"Is your cousin, Berkshire, from Switzerland?"

"Oh, no," Barni said hastily. "Our family is of German descent, or rather Austrian. My father was born in Innsbruck, of a big family. He had five brothers and three sisters. He left Innsbruck and came to Interlaken when he was out of school. Berkshire is the son of my father's sister, who married a Berlin German who was a politician, a customs employee. Hans is their only child. He grew up in Germany."

Barni smiled, "I'm rambling, aren't I? I guess the words come out of me because I'm nervous."

"How did you get mixed up in this?" Pat asked curiously.

"Oh, I wrote an article for a Swiss magazine, a sort of anti-Nazi article, and Hans saw it in Berlin," Barni explained. "He wrote me. We corresponded. Then Hans came to see me, and it developed that he wanted me to help out in an anti-Nazi organization. He wanted a Swiss clearing-house for his group. I hate Nazis. So I was willing."

"Was it interesting?"

"In a way. Not exciting. Men and women would come to me, and leave packages or messages or money, and others would pick them up. I was sort of a middle-man."

"There's nothing dull about the present situation," Pat reminded her.

"No. This just started four days ago. Hans arrived in Switzerland in a wild state of nerves, and wanted me to come to Portugal and help him on this affair. I did."

"And that's all?"

"That's all. The first real work I did for Hans was tonight, when he sent me to learn whether Doc Savage was really Doc Savage. I was doing that when I met you, as I told you."

Barni got up and went to the door. She tried it. She pounded on it with her fists, quick nervous beating that got no answer. She was much paler when she came back.

The two girls sat in silence. Each minute, Pat had supposed, and hoped, that she wouldn't get more scared. She was wrong. Her nerves were crawling. She would think of the blank-faced men, and stifle an impulse to be sick.

Barni asked, "What about you? You must lead an awfully exciting life, associated with Doc Savage."

"I'm not associated with him," Pat explained wryly. "I just barge in on his cases once in a while. I'm only his third or fourth cousin, not very closely related, although we have the same coloring."

"I supposed you were his sister, possibly."

"No, no, I was even born in Canada. Doc is from the States. I lived out in the wild west, what time I wasn't being educated to the eyebrows. My parents are dead. I met Doc when he was in Canada on one of his wild cases, and he sort of took me under his wing. I own a beauty shop in New York now."

Barni asked, "What about Doc Savage? Tell me a

little about him? I've heard of him frequently. He must be a remarkable man."

"He is," Pat said. "Amazing. He had a most peculiar youth. Something or other happened to Doc's father when Doc was a baby—I don't think even Doc knows what it was that happened. Anyway, it gave the elder Savage a peculiar fixation—that he must raise a son who would be a modernized Sir Galahad, going into the far corners of the earth to right wrongs and aid the oppressed. Sounds silly, doesn't it?"

"A bit unusual."

"Darned unusual. His father got a bunch of scientists to take over the kid's training. He didn't have a normal youth at all. A bunch of scientific experimenters had him from three-cornered-pants age up until he was old enough for college. They did their best to make a physical giant, a mental marvel, and a scientific genius out of Doc."

Pat grinned faintly.

"The funny part is that they succeeded to some extent. You'd think a goofy training like that would have turned out a freak. It didn't. Or at least he's not so much freak. He has his freakish moments, though."

"I've seen his pictures. He is very handsome."

"Save your time," Pat said.

"Why?"

"He's a woman-persecutor," Pat explained.

"What do you mean by that?"

"He doesn't understand them, and so he's scared of them, as nearly as I can figure it out. He has a long-winded explanation of his attitude. He says that he cannot afford a close tie with any female because the first thing an enemy would do would be to strike at him through her. That's just talk. The real reason is that he's so darned scientific he expects to understand how things tick, and he doesn't understand how women tick, so he's afraid of them."

"Maybe the right one hasn't come along."

Pat shrugged. "Several have been past. And some of them were pretty capable hussies."

Barni smiled faintly. "I think you are prejudiced."

"At least I've got you cheered up," Pat told her. Then Pat lost color—she felt as if she was losing nerves, control, courage, everything—and leaped to her feet. The door was being unlocked.

VII

Doc Savage came into the dignified old office asking, "Now what have you gotten into, Pat? Where's Monk and Ham?"

Relief hit Pat such a pleasantly stunning blow that she was speechless.

"You big ox!" she said, when she had words. "Why didn't you knock, or something, to let us know who you were. I like to died. They had us locked up in here."

Doc nodded. "Yes. To keep you safe."

"Monk and Ham are in a jam," Pat said, rushing into explanations. "They've been seized."

She poured out the story of how she and Monk and Ham had gone to the hotel, had encountered Carter, and how Carter had called in the blank-faced men. She explained how they had been taken from the hotel, and how she had jammed the handcuff links holding her to one of the blank men in the hotel door. She dramatized this somewhat to favor herself. Then she described the meeting with Barni, the escape of the zombie, and their ensuing troubles.

The thing Pat carefully omitted was any reference to the fact that she had talked Monk and Ham into going to the hotel in the first place, having sold them the idea of jumping in ahead of Doc and offering themselves as bait.

She tried to get on to the subject of Barni before Doc could notice that they might not have had any business going to the hotel in the first place.

57

Doc interrupted her with, "Why did the three of you go back to the hotel?"

"Why," Pat said, "it seemed a natural thing to do."

"What was natural about it?"

"Well—"

"You knew the place would be watched."

"But—"

"Was it because you knew the hotel would be watched that you went back?"

Pat fell back on her usual methods when she was caught. She had found she could head Doc off by yelling at him. So she did some screaming. "Don't browbeat me!" she shrieked. "I'm doing my best to tell you what happened."

"Mr. Savage," Barni interrupted. "You shouldn't bulldoze Patricia. She has just had a terrible experience."

"Not as terrible as she had coming," Doc said sourly. "What are you two doing—sticking together against me?"

"Who's against you?"

"The Lord—I sometimes think—when he got that rib and made women," Doc said.

"Shut up, Barni," Pat said. "You get him stirred up, and he'll go to any length to get even."

Barni sniffed. "Mr. Savage, we are dealing with a situation in which a great deal is involved. I think I have some important information. Do you want to hear it?"

"Pat, who is this girl?" Doc asked.

"I was trying to tell you," Pat explained, and went ahead to describe who Barni was. "Barni had better tell you the rest herself."

Barni Cuadrado told, while Doc Savage listened intently, substantially the same story which she had told Pat. It had somewhat more detail. She repeated her own family history, giving that no more detail than she had given when she told it to Pat.

But of Hans Berkshire, she told more, particularly

of how her cousin Hans had looked her up after reading her anti-Nazi article in the Swiss publication. The enthusiasm of Hans, she said, had been intense and contagious. He was bitterly anti-Nazi, with a subdued emotion and intensity that one could not encounter without being impressed and fired.

Pat, listening to Barni talk about Hans Berkshire, decided she would be impressed herself by Berkshire.

"Mr. Savage, I am sure that Berkshire can help you," Barni said earnestly. "Will you see him?"

Doc nodded. "Naturally. With the greatest of eagerness." He looked uncomfortable for a moment. "Is there a chance you would accept an apology for the brusqueness a few minutes ago?"

Barni smiled. "Of course."

"When can we see Berkshire?"

"At once, if you will go with me. He is waiting."

Doc said, "All right. But will you two wait here while I explain to Mr. Dilling that there is no immediate danger."

"Will it take long?"

"Only a few minutes."

Doc left the dignified old office, closing the door behind him. The two elderly clerks were waiting outside, and he told them, "See that the girls stay in here."

The elder of the clerks nodded.

"Are they all here?" Doc asked.

"Up two flights of stairs. The second door to your left."

The stairway was ancient, with the dignity of another age. The second door in the second hallway had the same massive, timeless appearance.

Monk Mayfair and Ham Brooks were in the room behind the door. The blond man, Carter, was there. So were his friends, the men with the blank faces.

Monk asked, "How did it work, Doc?"

"Pat is scared."

"She should be scared," Monk said. He indicated the blank-faced men. "Our friends here are good. They even had me about half-scared."

Ham laughed. "Half? Boy, you were certain you were going to be a casualty."

The blank-faced man whose stern Carter had kicked rubbed the spot which had been kicked. "I was the casualty, if there was one."

Carter told him, "Sorry about that kick, Nick. I overdid it."

"It was a good touch," Nick said amiably. "That kick built you up as a Nazi tough boy, which was the part you were playing."

Mr. Dilling came into the room saying, "Sorry I am late. Did something go wrong?"

"The contrary," Doc told him. "We involuntarily netted a very pretty red-headed girl with an interesting story."

"Did we properly scare Miss Patricia?"

"I think so." Doc eyed the men with the expressionless faces. "You were fortunate to have such perfect talent on hand for a quick call."

Mr. Dilling chuckled. "Oh, they are quite an asset. We've been using them for a long time to frighten Nazis. Our bugaboos, we call them. We keep them on tap to scare Axis agents, and they have done several fine jobs for us."

The blank-faced man who had been kicked said, "This was one of our less skillful efforts. We had rather short notice, very little time to plan those pretended efforts to take Miss Patricia's life."

"It's a good thing she didn't question the waiter in the sidewalk cafe closely," another zombie said. "The fellow wasn't any too bright, and he wouldn't have fooled Miss Savage long if she had waited to grill him."

Another blank-faced man said, "And I was very stupid, the way I let her get my handcuff chain wedged in the hotel door."

Monk said, "That wasn't your fault. Pat thinks fast."

"The point is," interrupted Mr. Dilling, "did we frighten Miss Savage into going back to New York?"

"With another little push," Doc said, "she might do it."

"I'll help you give the push," Mr. Dilling offered. "This thing is really too dangerous for a young woman."

"I'll let you push her," Doc told him. "But first, there is a red-headed girl named Barni Cuadrado who has a story."

He told them Barni Cuadrado's story, using his own words to shorten the story, but managing to omit no details.

Mr. Dilling was excited. "Jove! We'd better move quickly on that."

Doc indicated Monk and Ham and the blank-faced men, "These fellows will have to keep out of sight. Monk and Ham are supposed to be kidnapped. And these other fellows are supposed to be their kidnappers."

Monk showed alarm.

"Now wait a minute!" the homely chemist exploded. "If you think Ham and I are going back to New York with Pat—"

"Wait a minute," Doc interposed. "Nobody said anything about your going back to New York. What I want you to do is this: Follow me out to the place where we are to meet this Hans Berkshire. Keep out of sight. But be ready to help."

Monk was relieved. "Sure."

Carter asked, "Does that include us?"

"Better not," Doc said, "for more than one reason. First, a few of us may be able to do more than many. Second, since you fellows have been scaring Nazis, some of the Nazis may know who you are. Third, there may be a chance of making the Fuehrer's gang of insiders think you are a mysterious unattached group of enemies. In that last role, you may be very useful later."

"That's logical," Mr. Dilling said. "Carter, you and

your friends keep out of it." He turned to Doc. "Mr. Savage, you and your two men will proceed alone. Is that it?"

"Yes."

"Good."

"Would you care to throw a final scare into Pat now?" Doc asked.

"Just watch me," Mr. Dilling said.

Doc Savage would have sworn Mr. Dilling's face was pale when they went in to confront Pat and Barni. Mr. Dilling was a marvelous actor.

He began telling Pat how lucky she had been to escape alive. The tone he used, and his concern, his intensity, was calculated to cause a bad case of cold chills. It did.

"For some reason, they have marked you particularly for death," Mr. Dilling told Pat. "Can you think of any reason? Any particular reason?"

Pat couldn't.

"They must think you have stumbled on to some very vital fact," Mr. Dilling continued. "Think. Wrack your brain. Can't you think of anything?"

"Not a thing," Pat said. "I've told Doc everything."

"Well, they must believe you have discovered something you haven't."

"That could be."

Mr. Dilling did some alarmed clucking. Then he proceeded to tell Pat that the blank-faced men were a very tough, clever and sinister group. Mysterious fellows. Mr. Dilling gave the impression plainly that he could not assume to protect Pat.

Doc became alarmed, because Mr. Dilling was piling it on with a shovel.

"Here is what we will do to get them off your trail," Mr. Dilling told Pat. "We will put you aboard a Clipper plane leaving immediately for North Africa. At the first stop, you will get off, ride back, and we will meet you to be sure they are no longer on your trail."

Pat surprised Doc by not objecting. He could see that she was scared. He wished that he had Mr. Dilling's ability to tell such bald-faced lies in such alarming fashion.

They loaded into automobiles which Mr. Dilling had conveniently on hand.

Doc told Barni, "We will get Pat aboard this plane. Then I will go with you."

Barni agreed.

They drove to the Clipper landing station, found a ship with the motors running and the attendants waiting impatiently.

Pat was rushed down the gang-plank, flanked by an impressive armed guard, and popped into the plane.

"Oh, Doc," she wailed. "That old gun of mine—I hate to be foolish about it, but I wish you'd look for it. Will you, or send someone to search for it?"

"Sure," Doc said.

The plane took off.

Monk asked curiously, "Doc, what became of her artillery?"

"In my pocket."

"Then why didn't you give—"

Doc glanced at Monk queerly. "Monk, don't tell anyone I have that gun. And tip Ham off not to tell anyone."

Monk was puzzled. "Sure. But what bearing could that old gun have on anything?"

Doc hesitated, started to speak, then said hastily, "I'll tell you later. Here comes Dilling."

Mr. Dilling arrived wiping his face with a handkerchief and asking, "How did you like that for a send-off?"

"Africa is hardly more than an hour or two flying—"

"She isn't going to Africa, because the plane isn't going to Africa," said Mr. Dilling smugly.

"No?"

"No indeed. That plane is headed for New York, and the pilot, who is incidentally a tough cookie, was informed that all kinds of hell would break around his ears if the young lady didn't make the full trip to New York."

"Then you think Pat is on her way to New York, willing or no?"

"I know so," said Mr. Dilling emphatically.

"And I hope so," Doc told him.

"Would you mind telling me," said Mr. Dilling, "whether you usually have this much trouble discouraging her when she makes up her mind to enlist as one of your assistants?"

"This," Doc assured him, "was one of the milder instances."

Doc moved toward the street. He took off his hat and examined it intently, then put it back on—this being an old signal meaning that his aides should let him know, but not too obviously, whether they were around. Shortly he saw Monk show himself. Monk and Ham were keeping track of him, but in the background, as instructed.

Mr. Dilling said, "You can use this roadster."

The car was an old Italian one, good as automobiles went in Europe these days. Doc loaded Barni into it.

"All right, now we can see Berkshire," he told her.

VIII

It did not take Doc many blocks of driving to realize that he still had uneasiness about Pat. It was a sullen, vague unsureness, and he finally decided it was spawned by a doubt that Pat had been taken in by Mr. Dilling's bald-faced lying. He put the uneasiness away, stopped letting it plague him. What if Pat did discover Mr. Dilling had been telling whoppers? There was nothing she could do about it. Or was there?

"You have," said Barni Cuadrado, "the expression of a man about to eat a grasshopper."

"That," Doc admitted, "paints a good word picture."

"You were thinking of Patricia?"

"Yes."

"She will be safe now."

"That wasn't the point. What was bothering me was whether I could depend on being safe from her."

Barni glanced at him pleasantly and said, "You shouldn't abuse Pat. She thinks you're wonderful."

"I think she's wonderful, too," Doc said. "She can get my plans balled up worse in five minutes than most people can in a week. Frequently she makes things come out all right, which is bad. If she were dumb, and nothing she did worked, it wouldn't be so disconcerting. Anyway, she is safer out of this thing. This is a very big thing. Somebody will probably get hurt before it is over. It is nothing for a woman. Which brings me around to the fact that we are going to put you someplace where it is safe as soon as I talk to Berkshire."

65

"You expect me to object to that, don't you?"

"Well, I wouldn't say, because I don't know you very well."

"I'm going to surprise you. I won't object. I'm scared stiff, and I don't like it. The sooner I'm out of it, the better."

"Where do we turn?"

"Several blocks on," she said.

He drove rapidly enough to give the appearance of being in a hurry, but doing some unnecessary gear shifting and getting caught in traffic jams wherever he could, in order to give Monk and Ham an easier time of following him. There was a gray car trailing him. He hoped it carried Monk and Ham.

She was pretty. Barni Cuadrado—she didn't look Spanish or Italian, but the name was one or the other. Swiss, of German stock, she was supposed to be. The red hair looked amply Nordic, and so did her features. Her features were very fine, her eyes a cerulean blue that made him think of the Gulf Stream off Bimini.

She was wearing, he realized with surprise, no makeup that he could detect. He had never seen a girl quite so plain darned pretty without makeup.

Boy, she looked like a million in shining pennies.

And boy, he'd better get his mind on something else. He'd better turn his little cart around and hike.

"I wish you weren't as pretty as Christmas morning," he said.

She laughed. "I'll try not to live up to it. But you're not exactly something to scare babies, yourself."

He grinned. He felt foolish—which meant, he suspected, that he was a damned fool, because this was a time for dignity. This was a time when the fate of the world was at stake. It was a time when he should have his teeth clenched and his jaw shoved out, instead of wearing a simple grin.

He made a mental note to turn her over to Monk and Ham as soon as possible.

Monk and Ham were terrific chasers. He suspected they frequently saved him from making a lout of himself.

The house was on the strip of coast west of Oeiras, below Cape Roca. The region was possibly one of the most beautiful in Portugal, comparing favorably with the Riviera. It was a highly developed section, with fine villas, hotels and garden-parks, with the inevitable fine rich-looking casinos where the food was excellent, the music good, and the gambling on the hair-raising order.

The house itself had Moorish lines. It was rambling, beginning at the edge of a road and going up a hill in steps with terraces and patios that overlooked the sea.

It was not a small house. It was not exactly what Doc had expected, or rather it was definitely not what he had expected. This was rich. It was comfortable with that dignified extreme of comfort to which the rich, but only those who have been rich for a long time, become accustomed.

"You say Berkshire is a rich man?" Doc asked.

"I didn't say anything of the sort, because he isn't," Barni replied. "Why do you ask?"

"A man who has been very rich for several years comes to value certain things and care less for others, so that you get some idea of the man from his surroundings."

"You sound like Sherlock Holmes," Barni said.

Doc looked over the house. "Is there an army of retainers, or do we walk right in?"

"We'll find out," Barni said. "I have never seen anyone but Berkshire and a couple of old servants around."

"Does he own or rent the place?"

"I thought he—I don't know," Barni confessed. "Is it important?"

"Probably not," Doc said.

But a thing which arouses curiosity, he thought, is always important.

He saw no sign of Monk and Ham as he parked his car down the road a short distance and helped Barni out. But the two were probably in the neighborhood. They would know, from the way he had been driving that he was close to Berkshire's house, which would be their cue to be particularly unnoticeable.

Barni led the way to a small, iron gate in a stone wall. The gate, Doc noted, whether by accident or not could hardly have been built with more strength, and the wall was unscalable.

If you had a suspicious mind, he thought, it would be easy to conclude this place was a fort.

Hans Berkshire came through the gate grabbing at Barni Cuadrado with emotion somewhat more than cousinly. He hugged her and said, "I have been frightfully worried about you!" He managed to repeat that he had been worried about her four or five times in as many consecutive sentences.

Doc sized Berkshire up during this display. Berkshire was older than Doc had thought. He was, in fact, middle-aged, the appearance of youth being given by his athletic body and the way he wore his hair, his clothing. The flaming red hair helped the effect of electric energy.

He was very tweedy. His suit cloth was brown and coarse. His cane was a heavy knobbed affair this time, and his gloves rough and brown.

The man was dynamic. He was pulsing energy and vital aggressiveness.

A fanatical anti-Nazi, Barni had called him. This man would be fanatical at anything he did.

Hans Berkshire swung to Doc Savage, saying, "Pardon me, sir, but you are Doc Savage, I presume? I was very worried about Barni. I should never have sent her on such a dangerous mission." He reached for Doc's hand. "But you are Doc Savage? I'm glad to meet you."

"We met before," Doc reminded him.

"I've been worried about Barni. I've been at my

wits end, although I probably didn't have far to go," Berkshire said.

He said it, Doc thought, as if it were a little joke he had learned.

"We met previously," Doc repeated.

"So we did," Berkshire agreed. "What became of the young lady who whanged me over the head?"

Barni put in, "That was Patricia Savage, Hans. She is on a plane for New York, for safety's sake." Barni sighed. "Patricia was very clever. She has brains enough for two people."

"That," said Berkshire, "is the kind of a girl I should marry."

This, Doc reflected, sounds like a broken-down vaudeville act.

He said, "Berkshire, I understand you wanted to see me."

Hans Berkshire smiled, looked as if he were trying to think of another gag, and couldn't. He said, "Have you any remote idea who I am?"

Barni said, "Hans, I told him who you are—that you are my cousin, that you are connected with a German underground group which is trying to keep Germany from being duped again by Hitler."

Berkshire looked relieved. "Mr. Savage, is there anything else you would like to know about me?"

Quite a few things, Doc reflected. He selected one at random.

"Just why," he asked, "are you calling on me for assistance?"

"Isn't it logical?"

"You belong to an underground group, as I understand it. Aren't they functioning?"

Berkshire leaned forward suddenly, dramatically. "Let me give you an American example: If a show was being produced in a New York theater with Benny Zilch for leading man, Benny Zilch being an actor of medium ability and no reputation, and someone like Bing Crosby turned up in town looking for a part in the same show—wouldn't the producers be fools if they didn't grab Crosby for leading man in place of Zilch?"

"Is that the situation?"

"Roughly."

"Who are the producers of the show, in this case? You, I take it, are Zilch. Who are the producers? Who wants to substitute me for you?"

"My organization," said Berkshire, "is a democratic organization. They all want you. If you are asking, do I resent your taking the lead, the answer is God, no! I am so relieved and pleased I could cry."

He looked as if he could shed tears. He hadn't looked that way a moment ago.

Doc said, "Where is this organization? I want to meet it."

"You will."

Doc, letting some unpleasantness get in his voice, said, "Now, I want to meet it now."

Berkshire grimaced. "I can't. They're not here."

"Where are they?"

"They are working."

Doc made an impatient gesture. "You had better tell me the whole story without forgetting anything."

Hans Berkshire was angry. His rage showed in the guttural German accent that got into his speech now. Earlier his talk had been slangy, almost American.

But he talked freely and rapidly. He described his organization, how it was made up of scholars and scientists for the most part. The type of people who hadn't been popular with the Nazis.

Berkshire deviated to dwell for a while on the subject of why his comrades had not been popular. They were brainy, thinking men, but their brains hadn't been the reason for their being in bad grace. The Nazis admired brains. The world might think not, but they did. It was because his friends had the ability to think for themselves that had put them in the doghouse, or was the reason for their going into the doghouse willingly. They had ideals. That was it. They had definite humanitarian ideals, and because of them they couldn't stomach the Nazis.

The organization, as an organization, had been in existence a long time. It had started as far back as 1936, in an informal way. Gradually the group had become a definite unit. They had started functioning in 1939, more as an organizing unit than as a working machine. They didn't actually do the work themselves, but masterminded it.

An example, Berkshire said, was the underground they had set up for getting Allied fliers back to England. None of the group personally met and helped Allied aviators, but they had organized—and financed—an underground setup which did. They had gone about it scientifically, taking their time and thoroughly testing the first underground, then when it was right, organizing others like it, profiting from experience.

Promoters was probably the best word.

Getting down to the present situation, the group had been rather fortunate in learning of Hitler's plans for himself in case Germany lost the war. They had naturally developed excellent pipelines into Hitler's private life.

How had Allied Intelligence learned of the Fuehrer's scheme to plant a double, flee, have the double murdered to make himself a martyr and enrage Germany into a last spurt against the Allies?

Berkshire's group had slipped Allied Intelligence the information. That was how.

Now Berkshire's group believed they knew where the Fuehrer was personally hiding.

He could be captured, but the group hadn't done it. The group hadn't done it, because they had a better plan.

If some British or American personality of great importance could do the actual seizing, the world would believe the genuine Hitler had been taken, and not some phony.

"The Germans," said Berkshire intensely, "have got to be convinced their leader was pulling a snide trick. They have got to believe it."

He leveled an arm at Doc Savage dramatically.

"If you take the Fuehrer," he said, "Germans will believe it."

Doc Savage was more fascinated than he wanted to be. He discovered that he was actually aflame with impatience and excitement, that he was filled with a rattlebrained ardor of the sort he usually managed to avoid. This Hans Berkshire was a hypnotic speaker.

Doc, trying to be cold-blooded and careful, asked, "What about this house?"

"In what way?"

"Who does it belong to?"

"Me," Berkshire said. "I have owned it for about three years." He paused and looked deliberately shamefaced. "I bought it in a moment of fear that I would be found out and have to flee Germany. It was to be my retreat."

That was so logical that Doc lost all ability to be hardheaded.

"There is no point in wasting more time," he said. "Why don't we get going?"

Berkshire asked, "You accept our proposition?"

"Naturally."

Relief made Berkshire's reddish eyebrows bunch together like pleased mice.

"That's fine." Berkshire consulted a platinum jeweled watch, an outlandishly expensive piece. "It is now ten o'clock. Dark. We will send a signal."

He went on to the highest terrace of the rambling house, where he placed a chair as if for reading, then put a floor lamp near the chair. He switched the lamp on, and it was a fluorescent lamp giving a bright daylight-blue light. He switched the light off after—he consulted his watch counting seconds—forty-one seconds. He switched it on again for nine seconds, then off, then on again and left it on.

"That will bring us an airplane," he said. "A seaplane, I imagine." He glanced at the sea. "Yes, it is a calm night, so it will be a seaplane, probably."

This was the first concrete evidence—other than the man's fluent talk—that Berkshire was part of a group. The idea that he could give a signal as simply as flashing a floor lamp was something Doc found creepy.

Doc pondered the signalling for a while. His guess was that they used number signals, and that the duration of the flashes—forty-one and nine in this case—was a transmission of the numbers. He asked Hans Berkshire about it, and Berkshire stated he was correct.

"How long will we have to wait?"

"That is very difficult to say," Berkshire said. "Some hours, I am afraid."

Doc stood up. "I am going to look over the neighborhood."

Berkshire nodded. "A good plan."

IX

Doc Savage left by going over a side wall—he checked carefully and found a metal rail along the top, supported on insulators, but it was not electrified, and he was careful not to touch it anyway. He looked back and saw the light on the balcony go out, saw the shadowy figures of Hans Berkshire and Barni Cuadrado go into the house. He went on.

Stillness was all about for a while after Doc Savage left. The quiet of night and the odor of flowers in the darkness, the drowsy whispering of the sea swell on the rocks below. The sky had a dappling of clouds and the sea was slick and silvery into the distance.

There a part of the darkness stirred and became a figure which joined another figure.

"Did he really go?" the first figure asked.

"Over the wall," said the second. "It would have been easy, so easy, to close the switch and throw power into the wall as he went over. That would have finished him."

"You cannot be sure of that."

"There is enough voltage—"

"He would not go over the wall without testing to see if the thing was electrified. He probably tested. And then he didn't touch the metal rail."

"Well, I didn't do it, anyway. Where did he go?"

"To find his two friends, I suspect."

"Monk Mayfair and Ham Brooks?"

"Probably."

The two had been speaking German, or rather

whispering German. There was more excitement in the sibilance of the whispers than in the text of the words, by a great deal.

"It would be so damned easy to kill him now, immediately," one said fiercely.

"That would leave Monk Mayfair and Ham Brooks."

"Well, we could get them later."

"Savage will bring them here, perhaps. Then it will be simpler."

"If he doesn't?"

"It will have to be arranged so that he will."

"We just wait, then?"

"Not exactly. You do not, anyway."

"Eh?"

"You will proceed immediately to Vimeiro, and get aboard our power launch. The password is April Seventeenth. You will pick up Patricia Savage."

"So they got her?"

"They are getting her," the other said. "You had better be moving."

The two figures separated. One left the house furtively.

The Clipper had been flying less than an hour, and Pat had discovered that it wasn't headed for Africa, and asked the pilot what was what. The pilot told her to go back and sit down, which was the wrong thing to tell Pat, particularly in a smug, you've-been-slicked tone.

"I've been flim-flammed!" Pat said grimly.

"You're just being taken to New York, is all."

"At whose orders?"

"Doc Savage's."

Pat did some thinking, a quick adding of two and two, and decided that she had been elaborately taken in. It was characteristic of Pat that once she smelled one rat, everything and everybody looked like rats.

She concluded the blank-faced men had been working for Doc, the attempts on her life had been fakes, and for good measure she decided Barni Cuadrado was probably a stooge of Doc's. She remembered how scared she had been, and she pulled out the cork and said what she thought. There was no one to say it to but the clipper pilot, who was a freckled young man who seemed to enjoy seeing a pretty girl get mad.

Pat didn't use anything that was profanity, technically, but she got enough words out of the dictionary to make her feelings plain. She included an opinion of the freckled pilot's character and antecedents.

"That's great," said the pilot. "That's as expertly as I ever heard nice words used to remove hide and feathers. Now do you feel better?"

Pat went back and sat down. She would probably wind up in New York, and there was nothing she could do about it.

She became downcast. Probably, she thought, she should be ashamed of herself for causing Doc Savage so much trouble. She had not helped Doc's effort by getting, or trying to get, into the excitement. The only result had been that Doc had been forced to take time off to trick her into going back to New York.

I'm a miserable nuisance, she reflected. I don't help. I make Doc mad. I take up his time. I don't do a bit of good. I should stick with the beauty shop business.

She was in this sour mental state, and was as near making a decision to forget excitement as she had ever been, when a shuddering, not too violent, seized the plane for a moment.

She looked about, and discovered two of the passengers staring in horror at one of the wings. They were looking at a series of ragged bullet holes.

Pat, alarmed, made a rush for the control compartment, demanding, "What's happening?"

The pilot was busy swiveling his neck to look at

the sky and he said, apparently not having heard her, "Here he comes again!"

Pat followed his eyes, and discovered another plane. The plane looked distant, small and black. She had never been in an air dogfight, so she didn't realize how an attacking plane would look. This one seemed far off and harmless.

But the other plane came down the sky like a black wasp on a string, having more than twice the airspeed of the Clipper, apparently. Red fires appeared briefly along its wing edges. The tracer sparks floated past in front of the Clipper.

The co-pilot suddenly clapped his palms against the radio headphones. "You hear that? Hell, he's speaking English."

The pilot nodded.

"We better do it," he said.

"Do what?" Pat screamed at them.

"Land. Get back in your seat," the pilot said.

She had no intention of going back to her seat, but the co-pilot turned and shoved her out of the control compartment, yanked the door shut and latched it.

Pat went back and sat down. She saw the dark ship flash past, and got a look at the cross on its fuselage. Nazi. A Blohm and Voss HA 140, she decided. It didn't have twice the speed of the Clipper, after all. But it had enough.

She watched the Nazi ship roll and come back, a nasty streamlined thing with its twin rudder fins.

Then the co-pilot was at Pat's elbow.

"We've got a little choice for you to make," he said. His face was gray and sick.

Pat stared at him. She suddenly felt gray herself.

"They want you," the co-pilot said.

"Me?"

"Yes. Here's the situation. They tell us over the radio if we'll land and put you aboard their ship, they'll let us go. If not, they'll shoot us down."

Pat saw what he meant. There were about fifteen other passengers aboard the Clipper, four of them women. It was one or fifteen.

"I'll get off," she said. "And don't look so white-faced about it."

The co-pilot swallowed a couple of times. He muttered, "Sorry I shoved you around a while ago. I'll go tell the pilot."

The Clipper began a slow spiral toward the sea. Pat, looking down anxiously, decided that the sea was smooth enough that the Clipper could land and take off safely. In fact, the sea was remarkably without its usual squirming swell. There were waves, but they were small, like the waves on a pond.

She couldn't see the HA 140, but she knew it must be circling above.

The Clipper pilot made a good landing. There was some shock and splash.

Pat went forward.

The radioman put his head out of his cubby and said, "I slammed plenty of power into the radio during the talk with the Fritzes. The mainland probably picked it up. It may not do any good."

"Thanks," Pat said.

The pilot and co-pilot were tussling with a bulky bundle.

"Life-raft," the pilot explained. "We're supposed to put you afloat on it, and leave you. You and your baggage."

"That's a great future," Pat said, and then wondered how she could say something that silly when she was so scared.

The pilot told her, "We'll circle back past here in half an hour or so, and if they're not around, we'll pick you up. Or do you want us to?"

"You're darn right I want you to," Pat told him fervently.

"Okay. I didn't know what was going on here."

"Neither do I," Pat said.

They put the raft into the water, and helped Pat into the thing. It was a conventional life raft carried by planes at sea.

The co-pilot showed her a container of small packages. "Sea trace," he explained. "Colors the water, so another plane can see you from the air. Use it if you're here when we come back."

"Thanks."

"And if they start machine-gunning you, just stick below the surface and stay down. Bullets won't go far into the water, and they can only fire bursts that are short. In one dive, they won't be able to shoot at you for more than twenty seconds, probably. You can stay under that long."

Pat watched them climb back into the Clipper, watched the Clipper, looking as big as a house and as safe as home and mother, move away, gather speed, take off. She gave her attention to the Nazi.

The HA 140 was orbiting slowly in the sky above. The pilot waited all of five minutes, until the Clipper, as large as it was, became nothing but a sound as faint as a memory in the distance.

Then the Fritz came downstairs, squared off, cocked his nose up and set down. The ship taxied over to Pat's vicinity.

A bullet head popped out and screamed, *"Können sie hierher kommen?"*

"I guess I can," Pat said. They wanted to know if she could come there. She began to paddle with the folding oar that had been in the raft.

The man in charge of the torpedo bomber was a hard brown fellow with fox ears, moist eyes and the most polite manner Pat had encountered in a long time.

"Wie geht es Ihnen, fräulein," he said.

And when Pat said, "How about some English?" he smiled and said, "Ach, I vill do mine pest, but I ham not goot."

He certainly wasn't goot. He sounded like a Katzenjammer Kid. He had more braid on him than an admiral—Pat stared, and her eyes popped. He *was* an Admiral!

Shades of little fishes, Pat thought, an Admiral. The first real live Admiral I ever met, come to think of it, and that is something, even if he is a Fritz Admiral.

"You are goot enough, Admiral," she told him. "Now what goes on?"

He said, with great politeness, "I vas to get you, fräulein. Beyond dot, I know nottings. Is dot all your baggage?"

Brother, that accent is precious, Pat nearly said. But she kept the words back. "That's all my baggage —a handbag."

The HA 140 bounced around on what swell there was, and did a none too good job of getting off. The sea is not the best landing for a seaplane even on the calmest of days, and the smaller the plane the worse the prospects. This one, although it wasn't exactly small, was none too stable on its streamlined floats. Pat knew enough about flying to nearly bite through her lower lip during the take-off.

The Admiral was worried, too. She saw him wipe perspiration off his forehead. But once airborne, the plane climbed with a roaring abandon.

There was not much room in the Blohm and Voss. There is never much room in bombers, no matter how large the craft, and this was no exception. Pat had a small round iron stool on which to sit, and nothing to lean against. The only part of the outer world she could see was a small swatch of sky across which a cloud occasionally moved, and once the moon.

She sat there. They switched off the lights, except the infra-reds which lighted the fluorescent figures on the instrument panels. The two motors drummed with a heavy force, as if they were under the floor somewhere instead of out on the wings. There was not much vibration and only a little lunging in air currents.

Pat began to get a small feeling. Impressed, was another way of putting it. The Admiral did that for her, because, no doubt, he was her first Admiral. He wasn't a full Admiral, but he was part of a one, and even part-Admirals didn't go around personally forcing down passenger planes and taking off single passengers, unless it was pretty important.

She remembered that they hadn't searched her. Not even her handbag.

Hardly was that thought in her mind when the Admiral pointed at her handbag.

"You vill let me see dot, *nein?*" he said.

Pat let him see it. He went through the purse. He did it rapidly, and Pat could tell that he was looking for something, and that he didn't find it.

He looked up at her.

"You haff gun?" he asked.

"I haff not," Pat said sourly.

"Where is dot gun?"

"What gun?"

"Dot gross vun."

"Says which?"

"Big gun." He illustrated the approximate size of Pat's western type six-shooter with his hands. "Where is?"

"You want to know where my pistol is?" Pat demanded.

"*Ja.*"

"A little rabbit ate it," Pat said.

She spent the next hour wondering why in the dickens her six-shooter had become so important.

The ship was flying very high at the end of the hour. They came back and gave Pat a German altitude oxygen mask and showed her how to use it. She was slightly altitude sick anyway when the pilot throttled the motors down to idling, pulled on his heat, and began to glide.

They glided for a long time. The pilot, the Admiral, the other two Nazis in the crew were tight and nervous, watching whatever was below.

The change in altitude made Pat's ears hurt. She swallowed repeatedly, tried yawning.

Then, unexpectedly, the plane was on the sea again. It floated there, the motors still idling. Pilot and crew still had their tension. The pilot punched at a switch. Signalling, Pat decided, with his navigation lights.

The Admiral came back to Pat, squirming through the thicket of mechanism that filled the bomber interior.

"Where is dot six-shooter?" he asked.

"How bad do you want to know?" Pat demanded.

The German was no fool. He shrugged. "Dot is too bad," he said. He went away again.

Pat heard a motor. A boat. It came closer, drew alongside.

She was transferred from the plane to a snaky launch large enough to be seagoing, but built for speed of around fifty miles an hour.

The officer in the launch wasn't as polite. He was brisk with her.

"Where is your baggage?" he demanded, speaking good English.

"This is it," Pat said, exhibiting her handbag.

"You cross the Atlantic with only that?"

"I left in a hurry," Pat said.

"Where is the six-shooter?"

"Oh, nuts!" Pat said.

The officer demanded again that she produce the pistol, and she ignored him. The officer then went on deck, and shouted at the Admiral, in German.

Pat could speak and understand German, although she preferred not to use it. She was not particularly fluent, but she got what was going on outside.

The officer in the boat and the Admiral in the plane were quarreling about the gun. They were saying things to each other that weren't polite. Pat's first impression of the man in the boat was that he was a tough top sergeant—or whatever the equivalent would be on a boat—with no manners. But listening to him fuss with the Admiral, she changed her ideas. No sergeant would talk that way to an admiral.

The Admiral was supposed to have gotten the six-shooter and he hadn't, and he was being criticized. The two men finished off by giving each other a roundhouse cussing, then the boat got under way, and the plane took off.

The tough guy put his head down the hatch to glare at Pat.

"You are in bad trouble," he said.

Then he switched out the lights, and went to the wheel. The boat stuck its nose up, climbed half out of the water, and made knots.

X

There was some trace of daylight in the eastern sky when the speedboat snugged up against the old truck tires which served as fenders on a float in a small bay.

Pat was bustled off the craft. A man seized each of her arms. Another man was all ready with wide adhesive tape and he clapped it over her mouth before she knew what was going to happen. After that, the best noise she could make was a loud buzz through her nostrils.

The two who had her arms ran her up a path that twisted up the face of a near cliff. The tough fellow trotted behind her with her handbag.

At the hilltop, she changed hands again.

This time, she nearly shrieked with relief.

"Mr. Carter!" she nearly cried.

But Mr. Carter caught her eye and made, with seeming casualness, a gesture of dragging at the cigarette he was smoking. And when he did that, he laid a finger across his lips signalling for silence.

Mr. Carter also demanded the six-shooter. He did it even more angrily than the tough guy on the boat had demanded it of the Admiral, and the outcome was about the same. The two fell to swearing at each other in German.

The parting of the two groups was extremely ill-tempered.

The tough man went back to the speedboat. Pat heard the speedboat leave the bay.

Mr. Carter told Pat sharply, "Get moving. You will go with us! And if you try to make a noise around that gag, it will be bad."

Pat had nearly forgotten the gag, which would have prevented her crying out Mr. Carter's name. He must have known that. So he had signalled her to admonish her not to let on that she recognized him.

They began walking. Mr. Carter and Pat alone at first. Then they were joined by three armed men.

Two of the newcomers were some of Mr. Carter's blank-faced men, and the third was a shoulders-back young man who was obviously another Nazi officer.

They did not walk far, less than a kilometer, which brought them to a stone house, a pleasant place covered with vines and with bright blue shutters. Pat was taken into a large room which had a fireplace and pleasant furniture.

"I will question the *fräulein*," Mr. Carter told the others. "Leave us alone. Go outside and keep a sharp lookout."

The others left.

When they were alone, Mr. Carter dropped his voice and said urgently, "You mustn't let on that you know me. Keep on pretending, as you have been. It is very important."

Pat gurgled, pulled at the tape on her lips. Mr. Carter helped her undo it, warning, "Very quiet, please!" Getting the tape off was agonizing.

"What on earth are you doing here?" Pat gasped, when she could speak.

"I am very sorry I did not take you and Mr. Savage into my confidence before," Mr. Carter said. "As a matter of fact, I am supposed to be a German agent."

"But you—Mr. Dilling said you and those—those men with the blank faces—were working for him."

"That's my real job."

"I don't—"

"It's a bit confusing," said Mr. Carter. "First, let

me say that I am a Dane by nationality, and I do not like Nazis. There was a time when I was not intelligent enough to realize what Nazis were, and at that time I started doing spying work for them. My profession in Denmark was that of private detective, and at first the Nazis were just other clients for me. Later, I realized the kind of fellows they were, and I wanted to quit, but I was too smart to tell them I wanted to."

He sighed, as if the complexities of his past life distressed him.

"I came to Portugal to escape working for them," he said. "But it didn't work. They approached me here in Portugal, and told me to work for them, and threatened my relatives in Denmark if I didn't. That made me very angry, I assure you. So I went to work for them. But I also went to work for Mr. Dilling, who is an Allied Intelligence official."

"I knew that about Mr. Dilling," Pat said. "But what are you doing here?"

"I am supposed to get that six-shooter from you."

"Holy cow!" Pat said. "That six-shooter again. Why is it so important?"

"I don't know," said Mr. Carter bitterly. "I wish I did. Can you tell me?"

"I have no idea," Pat assured him. "It mystifies me."

"Where is it?"

"What?"

"The six-shooter. Where is it?"

"The Admiral got it," Pat lied.

Mr. Carter seemed stupefied with astonishment. "What did you say?"

"That German Admiral on the plane, the very polite one. He got it," Pat said.

"Why did he do that?"

"Darned if I know," Pat said.

Mr. Carter sat down in a chair. His knees seemed to be weak. "This complicates things," he said. He took his head in his hands as if there was an ache inside his skull. He sat there looking at nothing, and saying nothing, although his lips moved frequently without sound. Pat decided he was swearing to himself.

"That damned Admiral," Mr. Carter said finally, "must have taken a notion to look out for number one."

"Why would he do that?" Pat demanded.

"German Admirals, like German Generals and bigwig Nazis," said Mr. Carter, "are going to have troubles ahead of them, and they can see it. Germany has lost the war. There are going to be war-atrocity trials. A German Admiral will need influence. This one may figure he can buy influence with that gun."

"But why in the dickens is the gun so in demand?"

"I wish I knew, I sure do," said Mr. Carter fervently.

"What is going to happen to me?"

"I'll watch out for you, my dear," Mr. Carter assured her. "You will be safe. I will take care of you. I am supposed to get the whereabouts of the gun out of you, by force, if necessary."

"Who is giving you your orders?"

Mr. Carter grimaced. "I think they come straight from the biggest Nazi of them all."

"Where is he?"

"I wish I knew that, more than anything," Mr. Carter said fervently.

"Does Doc Savage know you are pretending to be a Nazi agent?"

"Not yet." Mr. Carter grimaced again. "You may have to vouch for me to him, if he catches me in what seems to be a compromising position."

"Where is Doc?"

"He's with that fellow, Hans Berkshire."

"And Monk and Ham?"

"They're with Doc Savage, I think."

"All with Berkshire?"

"Yes."

"And who is Berkshire?"

"Oh, he's really what he says he is, a German who is connected with a patriotic group of German anti-Nazis," Mr. Carter said sourly.

"You don't sound as if you liked Berkshire."

"I've never met him personally. He is bungling around in this thing, complicating it. But he may actually know where Hitler is. There's always that chance."

Mr. Carter lapsed into another spell of staring at nothing, holding his head, and muttering bad words in a low voice. Pat heard some of the words, and they were Danish. The Danish language seemed to have a very picturesque vocabulary of profanity.

Then Mr. Carter stood up.

"I must report on my attempt to question you," he said. "I will put the gag back on you. You must continue to look very scared."

"You going to tell them the Admiral got the six-shooter?" Pat asked.

"Oh, no indeed."

"Why not?"

"Because they might order me to kill you," said Mr. Carter seriously. "But as long as they think you may know where the gun is, my surmise is that they will have you kept alive."

He sounded as if he wanted to shiver. Pat felt that way, too. She watched Mr. Carter leave.

Mr. Carter closed the door carefully, after smiling at her, and locked it.

He met one of the blank-faced men outside.

"Go back and watch that female wildcat," he told the blank-faced man. "And expect anything. She is a very smart girl."

"Yes, sir," the man said.

They had spoken German.

Mr. Carter took a flower-bordered winding path to another house, a smaller one, about a hundred yards distant. Here there were three more of the expressionless men, one of whom was working on a portable radio. The other two were sharing a bottle at a table.

Mr. Carter poured himself a drink.

"That girl lied to me," he said sourly. "I know in my bones she lied to me, yet she did it so earnestly that I can't be sure."

"What was her lie?" one of the others inquired.

"That Admiral Gruehuntz took the six-shooter away from her and kept it for himself. As you know very well, that is a lie. Gruehuntz would not do that."

"Why wouldn't he?"

Mr. Carter made faces over his drink. "That is the hell of it, why wouldn't he? That is why I am not happy at all."

"You think Admiral Gruehuntz maybe did take the gun?"

"It is possible I am not thinking at all," Mr. Carter said bitterly. "Otherwise I would make more progress."

"Does the girl think you are really not a Nazi agent?"

"If she lied to me, why should she? That scares me."

"Did you tell her we were not Nazi agents either, but just pretending to be?"

"Yes, of course," Mr. Carter said, unable to remember whether he had told Pat that or not. "Yes, you will be as safe as I am, should Doc Savage catch us all."

"You think that will happen?" the other demanded, alarmed.

Mr. Carter swore philosophically. "I think it is impossible. Absolutely impossible," he said. "But here is the sensible other side of it. Doc Savage just possibly could come out on top."

He leaned forward and deepened his voice dramatically to emphasize that he was merely speculating.

"Mr. Savage has an international reputation, and a man does not get an international reputation for doing the things Mr. Savage does without having a certain ability," he said. "The point I am trying to make is this: Doubtless many other men have thought they had Savage in a spot where he could not possibly succeed against them. But he did. So let's not be complete optimists."

"When will Savage be finished?"

Mr. Carter said, "Savage and Berkshire and Savage's two aides, Monk and Ham, will probably start out to grab the Fuehrer very shortly. They have certain clues which will lead them, granting the devil sits with us, into complete extermination."

"What about the girl?"

"Her lease on life," Mr. Carter told the man, "is hanging by two threads. The six-shooter, and the fact that Doc Savage is still among us. She is also in the unenviable position that one thread will not support her continued mortality."

He was pleased with himself at waxing oratorical. The other man—they were speaking German—was a little confused. He was silent a while.

"If Savage is killed," he said patiently, wanting to get everything clear, "Miss Patricia will also be killed."

"Immediately."

"Would the other two, Monk and Ham—"

"Oh, they would have to be included in the slaughter," Carter said.

"And it will happen soon?"

"That's right."

The blank-faced man sighed. He had just one more question, and he put it plaintively, in a tone that had in it a little of you-have-dug-away-the-molehill-but-what-about-the-mountain?

"Who has got the six-shooter?" he asked.

Mr. Carter swore at him unhappily.

XI

Doc Savage had made his second trip away from Hans Berkshire's house. On his other trip into the night, he had found Monk and Ham, and told them to conduct a brief general investigation along any lines that occurred to them. Now he wanted to see what they had learned.

He found Monk and Ham under a tree, making a breakfast on sweet rolls and milk which they must have bought in the village.

Monk said, "I didn't find out too much. It's hard to find anybody to talk to that early in the morning, though, and everybody wants to talk Portuguese."

"You should have tried someone besides barmaids in the all-night joints," Ham suggested.

"That's a lie!"

"Well, who did you try?"

Monk said sheepishly, "Okay, okay, but it was only one barmaid, and a good idea, because they get all the gossip. I found out that Berkshire has owned the house three years or so, that he doesn't mix very much, but is a nice guy and fairly well-liked for a foreigner. He kicks in regularly to the local charities. His servants are local people, and he pays them well. He isn't here much. He is supposed to be a Holland Dutchman with a business in Lisbon that makes him travel a lot." Monk grimaced. "Fairly innocent picture, isn't it?"

Doc turned to Ham. "What did you dig up?"

"I was a little more scientific than my homely

friend here," Ham said. "I got the names of Berkshire's servants, and worked on them. They're a nice grade of servants, chosen for their ability as such. Most of them have been with Berkshire steadily since he bought the house, about three years ago. Berkshire is not there much of the time, only at intervals, and then for not much more than a week at the most."

"What about Berkshire's habits?" Doc asked.

"Okay, as far as I could learn. He speaks English, French and Spanish fluently, and Italian less fluently. He seems to have quite a bit of money, but he does not throw it around by giving large parties. In fact, there are very few friends as visitors at the house. The servants like him."

Ham frowned, digging in his recollection for other facts. "Berkshire likes American movies, and he has a sound projector in the house. He gets American sound films from Lisbon and has private showings of them. He runs the machine himself, and will run the American films over and over."

Monk said, "That doesn't sound so tough. The guy probably has movies for a hobby."

Ham nodded. "Well, there wasn't much more. The servants are all for him, as I said, but they don't actually know much about him. With a fine house like that, they feel he should get married and settle down. When Barni Cuadrado came to visit the place, they were as pleased as the dickens because they thought it might be a match, Berkshire about to get a wife. And that's about where the situation stands now—except that the servants think there's a little scandal around the house now, because Berkshire gave them, beginning yesterday, a week's vacation with pay, and told them not to come around the place."

"Is that the first time anything of the sort has happened?"

"Yes."

That seemed to be the extent of the news Monk and Ham had gathered. Doc told them to keep a sharp lookout, and be ready to trail him, or to give him some help if he needed it. Then he walked back to Berkshire's house.

Barni Cuadrado came flying down the path, her hair touseled, her eyes wild.

"Mr. Savage!" she cried. "A terrible thing has happened!"

She took him inside to listen to the radio. It was a good radio, and she had it tuned to the short-wave program which was being beamed to Spain and Portugal at this hour.

"He will be on again with the news in a few minutes," she said.

A moment later, the announcer in New York came on, giving the news in English. He talked about the gains in Europe, the progress in the Pacific, and some political stuff.

Then came the news that Pat had been removed from the Clipper enroute from Lisbon to New York.

The news seemed to freeze everything inside Doc for a moment. Then he broke the shock, faced Berkshire and demanded, "Where is your telephone?"

He got a man named Lander at the American embassy, and he didn't know Lander. But Lander must have been expecting his call, because he had information ready. He was able to tell Doc, in full detail, how Pat had been taken from the Clipper by a German bomber.

Lander said, "I am instructed to tell you that the Germans were very insistent that Miss Savage bring all her baggage with her when she changed planes."

"It was not just a routine request?"

"No, it was extremely insistent. They seemed to want Miss Savage's baggage as much as they wanted her."

"Which would make it appear they thought she was carrying something they wanted?"

"That would be a good deduction."

The embassy had no more information, so Doc broke the connection. He faced Berkshire and said grimly, "Look here, what are we waiting on? Why are we sitting here in this house doing nothing?"

Berkshire said, "We can go now."

"Why didn't you say so?"

"I intended to," Berkshire said mildly. "As a matter of fact, the messenger is just coming, so I could hardly have told you before."

He indicated the nearest window.

Doc Savage, gripping at his nerves, putting down rage and impatience and fear, went to the window. A man was coming. A young man, dark-haired and smooth-cheeked, wearing shorts and a light sweater. Berkshire introduced him to Doc Savage as Kinder. It was a nickname, obviously. The word Kinder meant child, so it was another way of calling the boy Kid. He looked like a soft, gentle, sweet character.

"The plane is waiting," the boy said.

It was a small plane as the world was in the habit of thinking of planes. This one was no bomber that had cost a million nor a transport that had cost hundreds of thousands. This one had cost not more than ten thousand dollars. It could carry a pilot and three passengers.

Berkshire explained, "It belongs to the boy, to Kinder. He does a little commercial flying from Switzerland, and is a great help to us."

The plane had floats. It was on a flat stretch of the river inland from Lisbon.

Doc asked, "Where are we going?"

"Switzerland."

"Exactly where in Switzerland?"

"Interlaken."

"Which lake?"

"The lower one, Thun. Or rather, the arm of it called Untersee, nearest Interlaken."

Doc nodded. "All right, one more question," he said. "Why are we being followed?"

Berkshire jumped violently, said, "Gott!" in a

frightened voice. Barni Cuadrado jumped visibly. The dark-haired smooth-cheeked boy became very still and looked at Doc Savage speculatively.

"I think we were followed. I could be wrong," Doc said.

"We'd better look into that," Berkshire muttered.

Doc said, "You three stay here. Better get out of sight and keep your eyes open."

He could tell they were scared. He knew that they had not known anyone was trailing them.

Undergrowth around about was fairly thick. Doc walked into it, going southwest, but immediately changed his course when he was out of sight, and went northeast. He walked carefully, silently, and shortly he found Monk.

Monk was leaning against a small tree, grinning. "They didn't see us, did they?"

"Apparently not," Doc said. "Were you two in that dilapidated Austin car?"

"That's right."

"Where is Ham?"

"He is down getting a photograph of the plane. We didn't know what might come up, and a picture could be handy."

Doc said, "Get hold of a plane. You had better get to Mr. Dilling in a hurry, because probably he can supply you with a plane. If you do it quick enough, and get a fast-enough plane, you can beat us to Switzerland."

Monk nodded. "Okay. Where in Switzerland?"

"Interlaken. Thun lake, the end nearest Interlaken. The neck of the lake is called Untersee."

"Anything more definite?"

"No."

"We'll get there," Monk said.

XII

It was a typical Swiss afternoon when they spiraled down to Lake Thun. At high altitude, they were able to see the perpetual glaciers and snow on Monch, Eiger and the Jungfrau, beyond the chasm that was the valley of Lauterbrunen. The clouds hung in layers against the peaks close to Interlaken, the lake water was crinkling and blue.

Barni Cuadrado gripped Doc's arm and said, "This is what I call God's country."

Relief was a tinkling in her voice. The red-headed girl was glad to get home. Doc studied her curiously, asked, "Your home is near here, isn't it?"

She tried to point, then said the hills hid her home. It was on the mountain above Interlaken, she said, on the north side of the stream.

The dark-haired boy was a good flier. He had army habits, and they were German army habits. The boy was Luftwaffe trained. He made a fine landing, shut off the motor and let the wind sail the plane backward toward a dock.

"Ever in the German air force?" Doc Savage asked the boy.

The boy thought about it for a while. Evidently he concluded that his Luftwaffe training had been evident. "Yes," he said. "I was in it. I deserted. How did you know?"

"Every army trains its fliers a little differently," Doc told him. "You show Luftwaffe traits."

"I'm not proud of them," the boy said.

He climbed out and jumped to the dock and fended the plane away while they got ashore. The spot where they had landed was a little boat-landing typical of the Swiss lakes. Nearby was a settlement, not large enough to be a village, three or four houses and a chapel and a general store selling everything from fine lace handkerchiefs to packsacks, wooden-soled shoes and cowbells of many sizes.

The scene was placid, rural, picturesque. The air was cool, pleasant, but chilly with a little of the zip of the glaciers on Jungfrau. There was the sound of running water somewhere.

The pilot extended a hand solemnly to Berkshire, said, "Good luck," in fair English. Then he did the same with Barni, with Doc Savage. His young face was solemnly inscrutable. Doc gathered he wasn't going along.

They started walking along a little road that was more of a path.

"The pilot know what's up?" Doc asked.

Berkshire shook his head. "No. He knows I am with an anti-German underground group, but that is all he does know."

"Where are we going?"

"There is an inn near. A car will come for us there. They will have seen the plane arrive, and send the car."

Doc frowned. "How much more of this running around is there to be done?"

"Very little," Berkshire said grimly.

The inn was made of logs and native stone. They had dark coffee and rich cakes on the terrace. Berkshire seemed nervous, expectant, while Barni was less uneasy now.

Without being too obvious about it, Doc scrutinized the lake for some sign of a plane in which Monk and Ham might have come. He didn't see one, and he was depressed more than was reasonably necessary. The lake was big, and a plane could be anywhere in a score of coves. Or the plane might have put Monk and Ham ashore, then gotten out of there, which would be more logical. But Doc was beaten down, a sign his nerves were on edge.

He was, he decided, aggravated with the way things were moving. Walk and talk, walk and talk. And all the while was the feeling that a lot of things were going on that were secret, mysterious.

Pat, for instance. How the devil had they known she was on the Clipper for New York? Going over that in his thoughts, Doc was sure that no one but Mr. Dilling and Carter and a few of their men, a very few, had known Pat was on the Clipper. Had the Nazis gotten the information from Dilling or Carter? Which one? Or had the Nazis seen Pat being put on the plane?

And why had they wanted Pat so badly that they had sent a bomber to intercept the Clipper? The Germans weren't in the habit of going after commercial planes on the New York-to-Portugal service in that fashion. For one thing, the Portuguese would raise billyhell about it. There had been a day when Portugal wouldn't have meant much to the Nazis, but that day was gone.

Why had the Nazis particularly wanted Pat's baggage?

"Berkshire," Doc said.

"Yes."

"You have agents here in Switzerland, haven't you?"

"Yes."

"Then why," Doc asked, "go to all this trouble to have me grab the Fuehrer?"

"It may be a mighty tough job," Berkshire said.

"You men aren't afraid of tough jobs. Not if you've gone this far with the thing."

Berkshire nodded. "That's right."

"Then why me?"

"I told you that before," Berkshire said. "The man who takes the Fuehrer must be an important man, a man the German people will believe. You are such a man. You, in fact, are the only one we could think of, who had enough stature. Just anyone could not do this, not effectively."

Barni Cuadrado said, "Hans is right, Mr. Savage. At first one would think that just anybody who captured the German leader would be effective. But this is a particular situation. The Germans must know we have the genuine man, in order to discredit the double who is now in Berlin."

Doc nodded gloomily. That was logical. And they'd told it to him before.

He shook his head at Barni Cuadrado.

"You don't intend to follow this to the end, I hope," he said.

"Why not?"

"Too dangerous."

She smiled somewhat thinly. "You haven't much of an opinion of my ability, have you?"

"I didn't say that—"

"Or are you just low-rating women in general?" she asked.

He was angry, and about to let her know he was angry, when a middle-aged man with a beard joined them and said, in German, *"Das auto. Werden sie gleich fertig sein?"*

The car was ready.

The machine was an old touring with the top down. Berkshire, with a violence that was unexpected, berated the old man for a fool and told him to get the top up and the curtains on. They lost time doing that.

Doc watched Berkshire, and saw perspiration on the man's neck, on his wrists above his gloves. The man, Doc thought, seems never to be without gloves and cane and that intense animal-aliveness. But the animal-aliveness was growing now, so they must be getting near the end of the trail.

"Is this going to be rough?" Doc asked.

"Probably very rough."

"Then Barni drops out now," Doc said.

"I think she'd better," Berkshire agreed.

"But Hans—"

Berkshire gestured impatiently, interrupted, "Do not argue, please. You will leave us and go home. It is close enough to walk, is it not?"

She tried to argue. "But I've worked for this moment—"

"Please do as I say!" There was an unexpected quality of authority in Berkshire's voice now, the tone and manner, somehow, of a man who had given many orders and had them obeyed.

Barni said angrily, "Hans, I am going to hate you for this!"

Berkshire shrugged. "I would hate myself if you got your pretty face shot off."

Barni gave up. She turned to Doc. "I don't know whether I will see you again—"

"You'll see him again," Berkshire said. "We will have a great celebration together when this is finished."

"All right." Barni extended her hand. "Until we celebrate, then. And good luck." She shook hands with Doc.

She did not leave, but stood there until the top was up on the car and the side curtains were in place, until the car got moving with Doc Savage and Berkshire and turned a bend in the road. She stood there until its sound had died below the tinkling of a small stream somewhere in the woods nearby.

Then she began walking. Her home was not much more than two kilometers distant, a little over a mile.

She did not walk far.

A man with a face as blank and expressionless as a cadaver came out of the brush beside the path.

"You will not shriek or otherwise cause a commotion," he said.

Barni stared at him in horror, because he was one of the men who had so terrified Pat and herself in Lisbon.

He shoved her a gun, cocked.

"Very still," he said, in German this time.

Another man came out of the shrubbery. He walked behind Barni and suddenly gripped her arms. A third man appeared, and slapped his hands over her person, yanked her handbag out of her fingers.

"You had better gag her," the first man said.

They gagged her. They put a roll of gauze in her mouth, a large roll which filled her mouth completely. Then, to keep her from getting rid of it, they tied more gauze under her jaw and over the top of her head. The man in charge approved the job. "It looks as if she had a bandaged jaw," he said.

Then he indicated the way the car had gone.

"We walk that way," he said.

Barni stared at him in horror.

"They are going into a trap," he told her gleefully. "A most clever trap."

They began to walk, holding each of her arms, one walking ahead. They walked steadily, purposefully, and Barni's heart seemed to stop within her and terror moved through her body making her fingers cold and the world like a dream to her mind. The walk was worse than she had imagined an experience could be.

The three dead-faced men stalked in silence, and she wondered what was the matter with their faces, what thing could be wrong that made them look as they looked.

But then they met a man and a woman walking arm in arm, the man swinging one of those steel-pointed canes which the vacationists buy to attach the little metal tabs they have purchased stamped with the names of the places they have visited. This cane had fifteen or twenty tabs, all new.

Barni's captors underwent an astounding change. They burst out in the expressions of men who were enjoying themselves completely, smiles, laughter, glad little gestures. And song. They sang a little song, kidding Barni's bandaged jaw.

Something about: "And she fell down, and she broke her crown—"

The two vacationists went on. The singers stopped. The deadpan looks went back on their faces.

Fear made Barni's nerves threads of ice, because now she knew the men weren't freaks. They weren't fellows with something wrong with their faces, and they weren't stupid. They were cold-blooded, clever devils. They were actors. Their minds were as quick as dynamite.

She was having difficulty walking. She had never imagined she could become that terror-stricken.

She did not know, at first, what stopped them. It was some kind of a signal, something they must have heard. They halted, waited, and Mr. Carter came down the path.

Barni felt a surge of relief at discovering the blond, capable-looking Mr. Carter. He was supposed to be an employee of the Allied intelligence. Surely he was all right.

He disillusioned her in a hurry.

"You're a damned nuisance," he told her sourly. He wheeled on the blank-faced men. "You got here with her all right? You didn't attract any attention?"

They said they had met only a man and a woman, vacationists, and had fooled them all right.

"Come on," Carter said.

They didn't walk far. Half a kilometer, the last third of it along a stony path, through a large arching stone gate.

Barni thought: I know this place. It is the old Basel family estate, and the last Basel, Joaquil, died four years ago. The place was sold three years ago to—her thoughts froze.

The estate—about twenty hectares in area, a lodge house, a little lake, a mansion of great size dating back beyond the Napoleonic war days—had been purchased by a rather mysterious person known as Mr. Fruice, an Austrian. A rumor had gotten around that Mr. Fruice was a different man one time than another—in other words, more than one man had introduced himself as Mr. Fruice. There was a little mystery about it. Nothing exciting. Just mild curiosity and gossip.

Mr. Fruice, decided Barni, was the German leader. Certainty poured into her mind. Everything checked. This was the hideout which had been purchased against the day when Germany would be defeated.

It gave her the distinct feeling of having walked out into an abyss.

They took her into the lodge house, which was a smaller building for the servants.

Patricia Savage occupied a chair in the large room. She looked neat, unruffled, composed, but there was a washed grayness about her face and a tightness around her eyes.

"So they dragged you into the show, too," Pat said.

Mr. Carter removed the gag from Barni's mouth. He said, "Screaming won't do you a bit of good. And it might aggravate us. Our nerves are somewhat on edge, anyway."

"Pat!" Barni gasped. "Why did they go to all the trouble of taking you off the plane?"

"So you heard about that?"

"It was broadcast on the radio."

"Oh." Pat was surprised. "Does Doc know about it?"

"Yes."

Pat grimaced. "I can imagine what he thought when he found out I was back in trouble again." She glanced up. "Where is Doc?"

Barni started to answer, didn't, and looked meaningly at the men to show why she didn't.

"I get it," Pat said. "Well, they haven't got their hands on Doc, at least."

Mr. Carter laughed. "Just give us a few more minutes, my dear."

Pat frowned at him. "You want to hear a little story?"

"Of what nature?"

"A story," Pat said, "about a mean little boy named

Stinky. He liked to smash up things. He used to get boxes of things out of the house and hit them with the axe to hear the noise and see things break. One day he got a box out of the back yard, got all set with his axe, and hit a lick. Only this time the box was a hive full of bees, and the bees were all over Stinky in a minute. Get the moral?"

Carter, in a tone uglier than any he had used so far, said, "Believe me, I am not in the mood for cleverness!" He turned and stalked off.

Pat glanced at Barni. "Did you get asked about the six-shooter?"

"The what?"

"The piece of artillery that my grandfather used to fight Indians with," Pat said. "It sounds ridiculous, but somehow or other the fate of Germany seems to hinge on the thing."

XIII

Doc Savage waited with Berkshire while the middle-aged man with the beard disappeared along a shrubbery-bordered walk, was gone a few minutes, and came back.

"The way is clear," the man said.

They went forward. They were in the grounds of a sizable estate. Below and to the left, Doc Savage could see a colored rooftop, and Berkshire had told him it was the lodge-house of the estate. But it was the house for which they were headed.

Berkshire said, "This estate was originally owned by a native family named Basel, but the last Basel died about four years ago. A year later the place was sold to a man using the name of Fruice. This Fruice was not Hitler, but a Hitler agent, his closest friend, and a man who is on this present plot with him. Another place, adjoining, was acquired for Hitler. He is there now."

Berkshire pointed.

"Just over the stone fence yonder," he said. "So you see, we are getting close."

The man with the beard took a dark pistol out of his clothing. He glanced at them after he did that, and his eyes looked wide, wild.

That fellow, Doc thought, won't be dependable in a tight spot.

He put the thought aside. It was not very important, put alongside the other things he had in his mind. He was tight, tense, with much the feelings of a man who had been hunting tigers, and now had come face to face with a sound in a bush that he knew was the tiger.

It wasn't any feeling of getting any nearer the Fuehrer, either. He didn't believe he was any nearer. Not a bit nearer than he had been in Lisbon, probably.

Rather, his tension, which was drawing and knotting until it was actually a pain, came from the certainty that his suspicions were true. He had told no one his real ideas about this thing, had given no hint as to what those ideas were. He had been secretive. He had pretended to be moderately gullible, not enough of a sucker to make it too obvious that he was pretending, and had gone along letting people think they had tricked him—probably some of them actually had fooled him, too—while he waited for the right moment. There would be a time, he believed, when things would cage themselves for a moment and a quick act on his part would slam the cage door.

It was nasty for the nerves, waiting. Man was made for action, and patience was not given to him in large quantities.

And it was particularly bad now that he was fairly sure what was what. Violence would come soon if his deductions were correct. They had, he suspected, a little more stage-setting, and then they would try to snap the trap on him.

He gave them credit for a great deal of cleverness. They were, if he had them figured right, going to chop just once and let that do the job. Which was good planning. One quick, complete massacre was a lot safer than a series of bushwhackings.

The old man with the beard went ahead again. He came back. He whispered to Berkshire. Doc got some of what the old man was saying by watching his lips. The old man was speaking German, and saying that they had better wait in the house a few minutes. But that everything was set.

"We had better wait in the house a few minutes, he says," Berkshire told Doc.

The house was majestic. It had been built back in the days when grandeur was man's god. But the furniture was poor, shabby. They scuttled across the hall and into a walnut-paneled place with a fireplace nearly as big as the room.

Berkshire got out his handkerchief and wiped the back of his neck again, his wrists above his gloves. He looked as if he would have liked to give one long, loud scream.

The old man with the beard arranged chairs for them. He moved casually, as if they were just visitors and this was any ordinary day. But his old skin was the color of a lead bullet and his eyes as wild as those of an animal.

They sat down. The old man was still there when Mr. Carter came in.

Mr. Carter was already making shushing motions with his hands, and he gave them a big-toothed have-confidence-in-me smile.

"I'm the last man you expected to see, I know," he said rapidly. "Now take it easy. Don't get excited. Let me do some explaining."

"How the dickens did you get here?" Doc demanded.

Carter grimaced.

"I'm afraid," he said, "that Mr. Dilling lost his nerve. By that, I mean that he became afraid you couldn't handle this alone. So he assigned me."

"But how did you get here?"

"Clues. Luck. I'll give you all the details later, if you wish. But right now—"

Berkshire was looking wildly concerned. "Who is this man, Mr. Savage?"

Doc said sourly, "He's a slick customer who has been working for Allied Intelligence for two or three years and hoping they won't find out he's really a Nazi man."

Carter looked hurt. "Really, Mr. Savage, that's not in the least kind."

"You're not a Nazi?"

"No."

"Want to bet?" Doc said skeptically. Then he added, "Or better still, want to look at something?"

Doc Savage fished under his coat and brought out an object wrapped in cloth. He unwrapped it, and disclosed Pat's ornate old single-action six-shooter.

Mr. Carter stared at the six-shooter. He lost color and his face lost shape.

Then he began screaming. He screamed, "Jon, Panke, Jacke! Come here!"

Then he made a convulsive gesture, evidently his idea of a very smooth way to draw a gun and make someone think he wasn't drawing a gun. "You mustn't move," he told Doc Savage.

Three men, probably Jon, Panke and Jacke, came galloping into the room, prepared for the worst. They were more of the men who could wear expressionless faces. They wore neat civilian clothes, to which they had added steel helmets—German army—and bullet-proof vests—German Luftwaffe—and cartridge belts and grenade pouches. They looked, with all the regalia, ridiculous.

Once the three were in the room, they didn't seem to know what to do with themselves.

Doc Savage was in a leather chair. Alongside him, but a little ahead of him, Berkshire was sitting on a straight-backed chair, crouched now, gloved hands fastened so tightly to his cane that the glove-leather looked tight. The man's hands had sweated so profusely from nervousness that the gloves were showing damp stains.

Suddenly Berkshire started to get up.

Doc said sharply, "Stay there, Berkshire! This is no time to move around!"

Carter said, "Savage, give me that six-gun."

Doc looked at Carter. "It's loaded," he told Carter.

"Five bullets. Forty-four calibre. Enough to blow a man to pieces."

He continued to stare at Carter, scowling, puzzled by his feelings. Fear—or whatever emotion last-ditch danger gave you—should be his biggest emotion right now. It wasn't.

His strongest feeling was one of elation at finally seeing through many things, at finally understanding what was going on and why. Actually, it wasn't exactly understanding. He'd had suspicions before. Now they'd checked out. His guesses had been right.

He had gone, he thought grimly, a little far into the thing before finally deciding that his ideas were correct. Perhaps too far. The next few minutes would tell that.

Still he could not, he thought quietly, have been sure earlier. The whole thing was a very cleverly woven net, with few things being what they seemed to be, and in a thing of this kind, he had to be certain. He was sure now. It was worth having to go so far into danger, to be sure. Even if he didn't come out of it, it would be worth it.

It was a difficult matter to sit down and decide you would give your life for something. He had never, honestly to himself, made such a decision. He didn't know whether he could. He doubted it. When a man was dealing with his own life, there were mental forces which were so practical that they transcended anything else.

"Sit still," he told Berkshire. "This isn't a time to move without thinking."

"Give me that six-shooter," Carter rasped.

Doc Savage didn't give him the six-gun.

He said, "Let me tell you two or three things, Carter. First, I am wearing a bulletproof vest. You will have to shoot me in the head when you shoot. You aren't sighting that gun at me, and shooting from the hip there is an excellent chance of your missing. If you miss, you know who I will kill." He frowned.

"If you start to lift that gun to aim it, I am going to shoot."

Carter sat very still.

"They say you've never shot a man," he said.

"Could you think of a better time for me to begin?"

Carter said nothing. He looked sick.

Doc Savage, in a flat emotionless voice completely apart from his more deadly occupation of watching Carter and the three men, said, "I had a hunch what Pat's gun meant, but I was not sure of it until she was taken off the plane and there was that report of her being ordered to bring all her baggage."

"Those attacks on Pat and Barni," Doc continued, "were a lot too realistic, the way Pat described them, to be an act. Pat is not inexperienced. And you knew too much about Berkshire, here, when you talked to Monk and Ham and Pat in the hotel room prior to the kidnapping which you were to stage. And the obvious effort to get the six-shooter from Pat—all of those things were noticeable when the story was told to me later. They didn't stand out. But they were in the story, and put together they had a meaning. Then, of course, when Pat was taken off the Clipper, the thing was obvious. You wanted the gun."

Carter said nothing some more. His eyes were small, crowded by the nervous bunching of his eyebrows and the knotting of his jaw muscles. He seemed to be completely uncertain as to what he was to do.

Doc asked, "Is this boring you?"

"Yes," Carter said. "But go ahead. It's giving me time."

Doc said, "Time is not going to help you. When you make up your mind to act, the thing is going to happen. Somebody is going to get shot. Europe will lose its bad boy, and Germany its leader. Or that will not happen. Depending on how the dice fall."

Carter's tongue made a pass at dry lips. "Go ahead and talk."

Doc said, "There isn't much more. It was an

accident, Pat's six-shooter becoming so important. A freakish accident, one that might never have happened. But it came out the way it did. And so you had to have the gun."

Carter frowned silently.

"What," Doc asked, "was the purpose of your elaborate business of decoying me to Switzerland?"

Carter said, "I am going to yell."

"You know the situation," Doc told him coldly, holding Pat's six-shooter in his right hand. "Do whatever you feel it is smart to do."

Carter shouted, "Kohl, bring in the other prisoners. But bring them in carefully."

The bringing-in was done most carefully. First came Barni Cuadrado, battered somewhat, her frock torn, with fright on her face.

Then Monk and Ham. Monk was in bad shape, although probably not as battered as he looked. Ham was less mauled physically, but he looked as if he was in more of a mental turmoil.

Pat was last. She was the most animated of the lot.

She said angrily, "Doc, they're after that six-shooter of mine! Don't tell them—" And then she saw the gun in Doc's hands. "Oh, you—that isn't my gun, Doc! You shouldn't try to fool them with a different gun!"

It was quick thinking on Pat's part. It sounded perfectly truthful when she said the gun wasn't the one, although it was a complete lie.

Doc shook his head.

"Easy does it, Pat," he said. "We have another hole card."

Carter said coldly, bitterly, "Savage, you miss the point. I'm going to tell my men to kill your aids *and* you if you don't lay that gun down."

As coldly, Doc said, "Go ahead."

Carter blinked.

"Go ahead," Doc repeated. "And I'll shoot your Fuehrer. I'll shoot him dead, and quick."

Doc's feelings got away for a moment. His own tension, mixed with contempt and hate—and an actual bloodthirsty murderous desire to kill—boiled up in him. For a few seconds, words and wildness came out of him without any real wish on his part.

"I'll kill him!" he repeated. "I'll make him dead, so much deader than any of the millions of people he's been responsible for killing." He added, between his teeth, in a voice he hardly recognized, "It'll be the most God-given pleasure I ever had!"

Carter looked completely ill.

Monk Mayfair became bug-eyed and asked, "You mean he's right here now?"

"Yes," Doc said.

The identity could belong to only one man in the room, and all eyes centered upon him as if drawn by a horrible magnet.

XIV

Much the same thought must have been in all their minds. There was no small fanatical man with a trick moustache in the room; no one resembled the man who had been born Adolfus Schickelgruber, son of an illegitimate father, in the Hotel zum Pommer in Braunau, Austria, at half past six in the evening of April 20, 1889.

Monk said, "But he speaks English. Hitler doesn't speak English."

He said it flatly, wonderingly.

Doc Savage—never taking his eyes from Carter or the others who were armed—said, "Didn't it ever strike you as strange that the German chief of state always made quite a public show of not being able to speak English?"

Monk blinked. "You mean—maybe he did?"

"What do you think?"

"My God!" Monk breathed. "It could be a disguise. But his red hair—"

Barni Cuadrado came to her feet then, as if something had taken her by the hair.

"Hans!" she said, and her appearance, expression and voice got sicker and sicker. "Hans, you are not what they say! Tell them!"

The man they had known as Berkshire sat very still. They could see that he had the build of the eccentric, screaming demagogue who had set Europe and the world afire. They could see that he had the

113

facial contours, the round ghoulish eyes. And the intensity, most of all, the intensity.

Barni brought both hands slowly to her cheeks, fingers doubled, and the fingers dug into her cheeks while her eyes became awful. "Hans! Mother of God Merciful, this mustn't be—"

Doc said, "He fooled you. But he has fooled the whole world at one time or another—"

Pat—women are essentially more brutal to other women than man is to man—demanded, "Barni, you said he was your cousin from Berlin."

Barni, around hands digging at her cheeks, said, "He—he said he—was."

"Didn't you ever demand proof?"

"No, because he talked of our uncles and our family so naturally." Barni's voice was going down into an ill soundlessness. "Oh God, how could such a thing happen to anyone!"

Doc Savage, in a cold intent voice that brought sanity into the situation, said, "I am going to shoot the Fuehrer if anyone makes a move!"

No one moved for a while. Then Barni Cuadrado made a low sickly noise like air blown into water through a straw, and slid down to the floor and lay there without moving.

"Poor kid," Pat said hoarsely. "Poor thing."

Ham Brooks said, "Doc, Hitler used the name of Berkshire and bought the house in Lisbon as a hide-out."

"This place here is probably a second hideout," Doc said. He glanced at Carter. "Or is it yours?"

"Mine." Carter's face was yellow.

"Just who are you?" Doc asked Carter.

Carter swallowed. "I managed the thing for him. I am his closest friend." He didn't sound as if he knew why he was talking.

Doc said, "Let's get the rest of it straightened out. The Allied Intelligence found out about this plot. They sent for me. Carter was doubling as an Allied agent, so he was able to pass the information along.

"Berkshire—to use the name we know him by—decided to handle the thing personally. He would meet me. He would make me think he was a German patriot—or kill me, if he had to.

"The first mishap was when he left his fingerprints on Pat's six-shooter. That was why he wore gloves all the time. He must have been afraid that, somewhere, someone would have a copy of his fingerprints."

Monk said, "Remember what Dilling told us? That Hitler had gone to a lot of trouble to have copies of his fingerprints destroyed in Germany as far back as four years ago? The guy had the fingerprint heebygeebies."

"Great grief!" Pat muttered. "Monk took his gloves off, and he grabbed up my six-gun without thinking and left his fingerprints on it! That's why all the fuss over the gun!"

"There were no prints on the gun," Doc said. "None you could identify. A gun almost never receives legible fingerprints, regardless of what detective books say."

"But they thought prints were on it."

"That's right—"

Carter tried his trick then. Carter started to turn away from them, then whirled back with his gun, his intention being to shoot Doc Savage. But Monk had been watching him. Monk was leaning against a chair, braced, set to throw the chair. He threw it with remarkable speed.

Carter cried out as the chair hit him, and upset. Monk went over, not seeming in a hurry at all, and stamped once hard on Carter's gun wrist. They could hear the wrist bones break. Monk picked up the gun.

What happened then could not have been expected to happen anywhere under any other conditions—unless the man who was the leader of German National Socialism was in the same room.

Ham took advantage of the situation.

Ham put back his head and bellowed, "Don't

shoot! Don't anybody shoot. You want to kill the Fuehrer?"

Monk calmly clubbed Carter over the head, making him shapeless on the floor.

Doc had hold of Berkshire by now. He didn't fool around with gentleness. He struck Berkshire, dazing him. Then he hauled Berkshire in front of him and jumped to a position in front of Pat and Barni, using the man as a shield.

Until now, during these first few seconds of it, it had been as if they were acting against drugged men, as if their opposition had no ability to think.

This changed suddenly. Someone said, in German, to throw down the guns, to take Doc and Monk and the others bare-handed. The command was followed.

The room suddenly filled with flying figures, blow-sounds, gaspings, scufflings, tearing of cloth, and the mewing noises men make when they are in a fight and being hurt. Monk and Ham were good at this sort of thing, and they went into it with heart and vigor. Doc Savage, after he had clubbed Berkshire, and slammed him down on the floor, told Pat, "Get hold of him! Hang on to him for us!"

Pat grabbed Berkshire and said, "You really mean this guy is Hitler?"

"He seems to be," Doc said.

Pat said, "This is the height of something or other," and she kicked Berkshire where it would hurt him the most. Berkshire screamed, and that helped to worry his men.

Carter was conscious, but in agony. He got an idea. "Get outside," he screamed. "We have them cornered! Keep them in this room!"

Why he could have them cornered any more with his men outside than he had now was a fine point. Probably his pain was such that his only thought was getting out of there.

The Nazis began going out.

Monk got a grenade bag away from one of them.

After about seven of them had gone out through

the door, Monk hooked the firing pin out of one of the grenades.

Monk was at his best in a hand-to-hand fight. He looked at Ham now, holding the grenade in his hand, and asked, "How long you hold these things before you throw them?"

Ham screamed, "Throw it, you fool!"

Monk tossed that grenade through the door. He flung three others as rapidly as he could pull pins and heave them.

The resulting devastation and uproar practically ended the fight.

Pat and Ham got Berkshire to his feet. The man was loose-bodied, without fire or spirit or will to do anything.

Somewhere in the confusion Monk said, "Ugh!" in a queer voice.

"What's wrong?" Ham shouted. "Are you hurt?"

"Carter. I started to pick him up," Monk said hoarsely. "His head—half of that last grenade must have gone through it."

"Let's go," Doc said.

They made it with an ease that was, considering the magnitude of the whole affair, an anti-climax. A let-down.

Mr. Dilling, the chief of Allied Intelligence immediately in charge of the Hitler-escaping-and-leaving-a-double-behind-to-be-martyred affair, did some headshaking in the little hotel overlooking the river in Interlaken that evening.

"It's God's wonder you didn't get slaughtered," he told them. "But what happened was undoubtedly this: The German Fuehrer was in that room, and his presence so overawed them that they couldn't fight."

"Couldn't fight—hell!" Monk told him. "You weren't there. They put up quite a scrap."

"But there were nine of them," Dilling said. "How you licked nine picked Nazi toughies in split-seconds, I can't imagine, unless it was that they were afraid to use their guns and grenades for fear of killing their leader."

"You're the guy," Monk told Dilling, "who put that Carter bird in our hair."

"I'll probably never live that down," Dilling muttered.

"You're danged right you won't," Monk said. "Didn't you know he was the Fuehrer's right hand boy?"

"Lord, no!" Dilling looked pained. "You sound pretty hot about it."

Monk grinned. "I'll cool down eventually. It came out all right, anyhow."

Doc Savage came into the room and asked, "Dilling, how is the international part of the mess coming now?"

"The Swiss?" Mr. Dilling grinned. "Oh, they are in an embarrassing spot. But they're going officially to know nothing whatever about it. In other words, if we get Hitler out of Switzerland and to England or America in a hurry, they will be very innocent. Nothing happened here, as far as they know."

Doc nodded. "You think the assassination of the double will come off in Berlin now?"

"Not a chance." Mr. Dilling grinned again. "In fact, we are sure of it. Word has come out by the grapevine that the killing is off."

Doc Savage was thoughtful for a while. He examined the floor, his own hands, feeling self-conscious and unnatural, tasting and feeling of an uncertainty which was still with him. The whole thing had been somewhat unreal. There were so many factors involved that he had not seen, that he did not understand, that he probably would never see or understand.

"Mr. Dilling," Doc said suddenly.

"Yes?"

"Is that man—that Berkshire—really Adolf Hitler?" Doc asked.

Mr. Dilling got a funny look. "It's strange, when things get so fantastic, how a man would give anything for one single truth to hang his hat on, isn't it?"

Doc nodded vaguely, as if the answer didn't exactly make sense. He said, "The girl, Barni Cuadrado, is going to need something like that, something solid enough to cling to until the shock wears off."

"How is she taking it?"

"Hard," Doc said soberly. "She is pretty much in pieces over the part she unwittingly played."

"You are serving as her doctor, aren't you?"

"Yes."

"You'll probably put her back together again," Mr. Dilling said. Mr. Dilling grinned slightly. "It should be a pleasant job."

Doc had an idea he was looking sheepish again.

A SPECIAL PREVIEW OF
THE SHATTERING OPENING PAGES
OF A NEW NOVEL OF RELENTLESS
TERROR

THE WOLFEN
by
Whitley Strieber

WARNING:

Here are the first pages from a new novel
that will frighten many readers. Do not
turn the page unless you are prepared for
a graphic description of the elemental ter-
rors that lurk unseen in the darkness of
city streets.

In Brooklyn they take abandoned cars to the Fountain Avenue Automobile Pound adjacent to the Fountain Avenue Dump. The pound and the dump occupy land shown on maps as "Spring Creek Park (Proposed)." There is no spring, no creek, and no park.

Normally the pound is silent, its peace disturbed only by an occasional fight among the packs of wild dogs that roam there, or perhaps the cries of the sea gulls that hover over the stinking, smoldering dump nearby.

The members of the Police Auto Squad who visit the pound to mark derelicts for the crusher do not consider the place dangerous. Once in a while the foot-long rats will get aggressive and become the victims of target practice. The scruffy little wild dogs will also attack every so often, but they can usually be dealt with by a shot into the ground. Auto-pound duty consists of marking big white X's on the worst of the derelicts and taking Polaroids of them to prove that they were beyond salvage in case any owners turn up.

It isn't the kind of job that the men associate with danger, much less getting killed, so Hugo DiFalco and Dennis Houlihan would have laughed in your face if you told them they had only three minutes to live when they heard the first sound behind them.

"What was that?" Houlihan asked. He was bored and wouldn't have minded getting a couple of shots off at a rat.

"A noise."

"Brilliant. That's what I thought it was too."

They both laughed. Then there was another sound, a staccato growl that ended on a murmuring high note. The two men looked at one another. "That sounds like my brother singing in the shower," DiFalco said.

From ahead of them came further sounds—rustlings and more of the unusual growls. Di-

Falco and Houlihan stopped. They weren't joking anymore, but they also weren't afraid, only curious. The wet, ruined cars just didn't seem to hold any danger on this dripping autumn afternoon. But there was something out there.

They were now in the center of a circle of half-heard rustling movement. As both men realized that something had surrounded them, they had their first twinge of concern. They now had less than one minute of life remaining. Both of them lived with the central truth of police work —it could happen anytime. But what the hell was happening now?

Then something stepped gingerly from between two derelicts and stood facing the victims.

The men were not frightened, but they sensed danger. As it had before in moments of peril, Hugo DiFalco's mind turned to a brief thought of his wife, of how she liked to say "We're an us." Dennis Houlihan felt a shiver of prickles come over him as if the hair all over his body was standing up.

"Don't move, man," DiFalco said.

It snarled at the voice. "There's more of 'em behind us, buddy." Their voices were low and controlled, the tone of professionals in trouble. They moved closer together; their shoulders touched. Both men knew that one of them had to turn around, the other keep facing this way. But they didn't need to talk about it; they had worked together too long to have to plan their moves.

DiFalco started to make the turn and draw his pistol. That was the mistake.

Ten seconds later their throats were being torn out. Twenty seconds later the last life was pulsing out of their bodies. Thirty seconds later they were being systematically consumed.

Neither man had made a sound, Houlihan

had seen the one in front of them twitch its eyes, but before he could follow the movement there was a searing pain in his throat and he was suddenly, desperately struggling for air through the bubbling torrent of his own blood.

DiFalco's hand had just gripped the familiar checkered wooden butt of his service revolver when it was yanked violently aside. The impression of impossibly fast-moving shapes entered his astonished mind, then something slammed into his chest and he too was bleeding, in his imagination protecting his throat as in reality his body slumped to the ground and his mind sank into darkness.

The attackers moved almost too quickly, their speed born of nervousness at the youth of their victims. The shirts were torn open, the white chests exposed, the entrails tugged out and taken away, the precious organs swallowed. The rest was left behind.

In less than five more minutes it was over. The hollow, ravaged corpses lay there in the mud, two ended lives now food for the wild scavengers of the area.

For a long time nothing more moved at the Fountain Avenue Automobile Pound. The cries of gulls echoed among the rustling hulks of the cars. Around the corpses the blood coagulated and blackened. As the afternoon drew on, the autumn mist became rain, covering the dead policemen with droplets of water and making the blood run again.

Night fell.

Rats worried the corpses until dawn.

The two men had been listed AWOL for fourteen hours. Most unusual for these guys. They were both family types, steady and reliable. AWOL wasn't their style. But still, what could happen to two experienced policemen on marking duty at the auto pound? That was a question nobody would even try to answer until a search was made for the men.

Police work might be dangerous, but nobody seriously believed that DiFalco and Houlihan were in any real trouble. Maybe there had been a family emergency and the two had failed to check in. Maybe a lot of things. And maybe there *was* some trouble. Nobody realized that the world had just become a much more dangerous place, and they wouldn't understand that for quite some time. Right now they were just looking for a couple of missing policemen. Right now the mystery began and ended with four cops poking through the auto pound for signs of their buddies.

"They better not be sleeping in some damn car." Secretly all four men hoped that the two AWOL officers were off on a bender or something. You'd rather see that than the other possibility.

A cop screamed. The sound stunned the other three to silence because it was one they rarely heard.

"Over here," the rookie called in a choking voice.

"Hold on, man." The other three converged on the spot as the rookie's cries sounded again and again. When the older men got there he slumped against a car.

The three older cops cursed.

"Call the hell in. Get Homicide out here. Seal the area. Jesus Christ!"

They covered the remains with their rainslickers. They put their hats where the faces had been.

The police communications network responded fast; fellow officers were dead, nobody wasted time. Ten minutes after the initial alarms had gone out the phone was ringing in the half-empty ready-room of the Brooklyn Homicide Division. Detective Becky Neff picked it up. "Neff," the gruff voice of the Inspector said, "you and Wilson're assigned to a case in the Seventy-fifth Precinct."

"The what?"

"It's the Fountain Avenue Dump. Got a double cop killing, mutilation, probable sex assault, cannibalism. Get the hell out there fast." The line clicked.

"Wake up, George, we've got a case," Neff growled. "We've got a bad one." She had hardly absorbed what the Inspector had said—mutilation and cannibalism? What in the name of God had happened out there? "Somebody killed two cops and cannibalized them."

Wilson, who had been resting in a tilted-back chair after a grueling four-hour paperwork session, leaned forward and got to his feet.

"Let's go. Where's the scene?"

"Fountain Avenue Dump. Seventy-fifth Precinct."

"Goddamn out-of-the-way place." He shook his head. "Guys must have gotten themselves jumped."

They went down to Becky Neff's old blue Pontiac and set the flasher up on the dashboard. She pulled the car out of its parking place and edged into the dense traffic of downtown Brooklyn. Wilson flipped on the radio and reported to the dispatcher. "Siren's working," Wilson commented as he flipped the toggle switch. The siren responded with an electronic warble, and he grunted with satisfaction; it had been on the blink for over a month, and there had been no response from the repair unit. Budget cuts had reduced this once-efficient team to exactly twelve men for the entire fleet of police vehicles. Unmarked cars were low on the list of precedence for flasher and siren repairs.

"I fixed it," Becky Neff said, "and I'm damn glad now." The ride to the car pound would be made much easier by the siren, and time could not be wasted.

Wilson raised his eyebrows. "You fixed it?"

"I borrowed the manual and fixed it. Nothing to it." Actually she had gotten a neighborhood electronics freak to do the job, a guy with a computer in his living room. But there was no reason to let Wilson know that.

"You fixed it," Wilson said again.

"You're repeating yourself."

He shook his head.

As the car swung onto the Brooklyn-Queens Expressway he used the siren, flipping the toggle to generate a series of startling whoops that cleared something of a path for them. But traffic was even worse as they approached the Battery Tunnel interchange, and the siren did little good in the confusion of trucks and buses. "Step on it, Becky."

"I'm stepping. You're working the siren."

"I don't care what you do, but move!"

His outburst made her want to snap back at him, but she understood how he felt. She shared his emotions and knew his anger was directed at the road. Cop killings made you hate the world, and the damn city in particular.

Wilson leaned out of his window and shouted at the driver of a truck stuck in the middle of the lane. "Police! Get that damn thing moving or you're under arrest!"

The driver shot the finger but moved the vehicle. Becky Neff jammed her accelerator to the floor, skidding around more slowly moving traffic, at times breaking into the clear, at times stuck again.

As the dashboard clock moved through the better part of an hour they approached their destination. They got off the B-Q-E and went straight out Flatbush Avenue, into the some-times seedy, sometimes neat residential areas beyond. The precincts rolled by, the 78th, the 77th, the 73rd. Finally they entered the 75th and turned onto Flatlands Avenue, a street of non-descript shops in a racially mixed lower-and middle-income neighborhood. The 75th was as average a precinct as there was in New York. About a hundred thousand people lived there, not many poor and not many rich, and about evenly divided between black, white, and His-panic.

The 75th was the kind of precinct you never read about in the papers, the kind of place where policemen lived out good solid careers without ever shooting a man—not the kind of place where they got killed, much elss mutilated and cannibalized.

Finally they turned onto Fountain Avenue. In the distance a little clutch of flashers could be seen in the dismal autumn light—that must mark the official vehicles pulled up to the en-trance of the Automobile Pound. The scene of the crime. And judging from the news cars careening down the street, the 75th Precinct wasn't going to be an obscure place much longer.

"Who's Precinct Captain?" Neff asked her superior officer. Wilson was senior man on the team, a fact which he was careful to make sure she never forgot. He also had a terrific memory for details.

"Gerardi, I think, something Gerardi. Good enough cop. The place is tight s'far as I know.

Nothin' much going on. It's not Midtown South, if you know what I mean."

"Yeah." What Wilson meant was that this precinct was clean—no bad cops, no mob connections, no serious graft. Unlike Midtown South there wasn't even the opportunity.

"Sounds like it's a psycho case to me," Neff said. She was always careful to pick her words when she theorized around Wilson. He was scathing when he heard poorly thought out ideas and had no tolerance for people with less skill than he himself possessed. Which was to say, he was intolerant of almost the entire police force. He was probably the best detective in Homocide, maybe the best on the force. He was also lazy, venal, inclined toward a Victorian view of women, and a profound slob. Except for their abilities in the craft of police detection, Becky liked to think they had nothing in common. Where Wilson was a slob, Becky tended to be orderly. She was always the one who kept at the paperwork when Wilson gave up, and who kept the dreary minutiae of their professional lives organized.

She and Wilson didn't exactly dislike one another—it was more than that, it was pure hate laced with grudging respect. Neff thought that Wilson was a Stone Age chauvinist and was revolted by the clerical role he often forced her to play—and he considered her a female upstart in a profession where women were at best a mistake.

But they were both exceptional detectives, and that kept them together. Neff couldn't help but admire her partner's work, and he had been forced to admit that she was one of the few officers he had encountered who could keep up with him.

The fact that Becky Neff was also not a bad-looking thirty-four had helped as well. Wilson was a bachelor, over fifty and not much more appealing physically than a busted refrigerator (which he resembled in shape and height). Becky saw from the first that she was attractive to him, and she played it up a little, believing that her progress in her career was more important than whether or not she let Wilson flirt with her. But it went no further than that. Becky's husband Dick was also on the force, a captain in Narcotics, and Wilson wouldn't mess around with another cop's wife.

The idea of Wilson messing around with anybody was ridiculous anyway; he had remained a bachelor partly out of choice and partly because few women would tolerate his arrogance and his sloppy indifference to even the most fundamental social graces, like taking the meat out of a hamburger and eating it separately, which was one of his nicer table manners.

"Let's just go blank on this one, sweetheart," Wilson rumbled. "We don't know what the hell happened out there."

"Cannibalism would indicate—"

"We don't know. Guys are excited, maybe it was something else. Let's just find what we find."

Becky pulled the car in among the official vehicles and snapped her folding umbrella out of her purse. She opened it against the rain and was annoyed to see Wilson go trudging off into the mud, pointedly ignoring his own comfort. "Let the bastard catch pneumonia," she thought as she huddled forward beneath the umbrella. Wilson was a great one for appearances—he gets to the scene wet, indifferent to his own comfort, concerned only with the problem at hand, while his dainty little partner follows along behind with her umbrella, carefully mincing over the puddles. Ignoring him as best she could, she set off toward the kliegs that now lit the scene of the murders some fifty yards into the area.

As soon as she saw the mess she knew that this was no normal case. Something that made you break out in a sweat even in this weather had happened to these men. She glanced at Wilson, surprised to see that even old superpro's eyes were opened wide with surprise. "Jesus," he said, "I mean . . . what?"

The Precinct Captain came forward. "We don't know, sir," he said to Wilson, acknowledging the other man's seniority and fame on the force. And he also eyed Becky Neff, well-known enough in her own right as one of the most visible female officers in New York. Her picture had appeared in the *Daily News* more than once in connection with some of her and Wilson's more spectacular cases. Wilson shunned the photographers himself—or they shunned him, it was hard to say which. But Becky welcomed them, highly conscious of her role as living and visible proof that female officers could work the front lines as well as their male counterparts.

Taking a deep breath she knelt down beside the corpses while Wilson was still registering his shock. Every fiber of her body wanted to run, to get away from the unspeakable horror before her—but instead she looked closely, peering at the broken, gristle-covered bones and the dark lumps of flesh that seemed almost to glow beneath the lights that had been set up by the Forensics officers.

"Where the hell's the Medical Examiner?"

Wilson said behind her. A voice answered. Wilson did not come any closer; she knew that he wasn't going to because he couldn't stomach this sort of thing. Clenching her teeth against her own disgust, she stared at the bodies, noting the most unusual thing about them—the long scrape marks on the exposed bones and the general evidence of gnawing. She stood up and looked around the desolate spot. About a quarter of a mile away the dump could be seen with huge flocks of sea gulls hovering over the mounds of garbage. Even over the hubbub of voices you could hear the gulls screaming. From here to the dump was an ocean of old cars and trucks of every imaginable description, most of them worthless, stripped hulks. A few nearby had white X's on the windshields or hoods, evidence of the work DiFalco and Houlihan had been doing when the attack occurred.

"They were gnawed by rats," Becky said in as level a tone as she could manage, "but those larger marks indicate something else—dogs?"

"The wild dogs around here are just scrawny little mutts," the Precinct Captain said.

"How long were these men missing before you instituted a search, Captain?" Wilson asked.

The Captain glanced sharply at him. Neff was amazed; nobody below the rank of Inspector had the right to ask a captain a question like that, and even then not outside of a Board of Inquiry. It was a question that belonged in a dereliction of duty hearing, not at the scene of a crime.

"We need to know," Wilson added a little too loudly.

"Then ask the M. E. how long they've been dead. We found them two hours ago. Figure the rest out for yourself." The Captain turned away, and Becky Neff followed his gaze out over the distant Atlantic, where a helicopter could be seen growing rapidly larger. It was a police chopper and it was soon above them, its rotor clattering as it swung around looking for a likely spot to land.

"That's the Commissioner and the Chief," Wilson said. "They must have smelled newsmen." In January a new mayor would take office, and senior city officials were all scrambling to keep their jobs. So these normally anonymous men now jumped at the possibility of getting their faces on the eleven o'clock news. But this time they would be disappointed—because of the unusually hideous nature of the crime, the press was being kept as far away as possible. No pictures allowed until the scene was cleared of the bodies.

At the same time that the Chief of Detectives and the Commissioner were getting out of their helicopter, the Medical Examiner was hurrying across the muddy ground with a newspaper folded up and held over his head against the rain. "It's Evans himself," Wilson said. "I haven't seen that man outdoors in twenty years."

"I'm glad he's here."

Evans was the city's Chief Medical Examiner, a man renowned for his ingenious feats of forensic detection. He rolled along, shabby, tiny, looking very old behind his thick glasses.

He had worked with Wilson and Neff often and greeted them both with a nod. "What's your idea?" he said even before examining the bodies. Most policemen he treated politely enough; these two he respected.

"We're going to have a problem finding the cause of death," Wilson said, "because of the shape they're in."

Evans nodded. "Is Forensics finished with the bodies?" The Forensics team was finished, which meant that the corpses could be touched. Dr. Evans rolled on his black rubber gloves and bent down. So absorbed did he become that he didn't even acknowledge the approach of the brass.

The group watched Evans as he probed gingerly at the bodies. Later he would do a much more thorough autopsy in his lab, but these first impressions were important and would be his only on-site inspection of the victims.

When he backed away from the bodies, his face was registering confusion. "I don't understand this at all," he said slowly. "These men have been killed by . . . something with claws, teeth. Animals of some kind. But what doesn't make sense is—why didn't they defend themselves?"

"Their guns aren't even drawn," Becky said through dry lips. It was the first thing she had noticed.

"Maybe that wasn't the mode of death, Doctor," Wilson said. "I mean, maybe they were killed first and then eaten by the animals around here. There's rats, gulls, also some wild dogs, the precinct boys say."

The doctor pursed his lips. He nodded. "We'll find out when we do the autopsy. Maybe you're right, but on the surface I'd say we're looking at the fatal wounds."

The Forensics team was photographing and marking the site, picking up scattered remains and vacuuming the area as well as possible considering the mud. They also took impressions of the multitude of pawprints that surrounded the bodies.

The Precinct Captain finally broke the silence. "You're saying that these guys were killed by wild dogs, and they didn't even draw their guns? That can't be right. Those dogs are just little things—they're not even a nuisance." He looked around. "Anybody ever hear of a death from wild dogs in the city? Anybody?"

These brutal murders are just the first of many violent deaths that puzzle the New York Police. Who are these mysterious killers who stalk helpless human prey? IF YOU ARE AFRAID TO FINISH THIS STORY, YOU ARE NOT ALONE.

(The complete Bantam Book is on sale June 20th, wherever paperbacks are sold.)

To the world at large, Doc Savage is a strange, mysterious figure of glistening bronze skin and golden eyes. To his fans he is the greatest adventure hero of all time, whose fantastic exploits are unequaled for hair-raising thrills, breathtaking escapes, blood-curdling excitement!

☐	11317	**MURDER MELODY**	$1.25
☐	11318	**SPOOK LEGION**	$1.25
☐	11320	**THE SARGASSO OGRE**	$1.25
☐	11321	**THE PIRATE OF THE PACIFIC**	$1.25
☐	11322	**THE SECRET IN THE SKY**	$1.25
☐	11248	**THE AWFUL EGG**	$1.50
☐	11191	**TUNNEL TERROR**	$1.50
☐	12780	**THE HATE GENIUS**	$1.75
☐	11116	**THE PURPLE DRAGON**	$1.25

FANTASY AND SCIENCE FICTION FAVORITES

Bantam brings you the recognized classics as well as the current favorites in fantasy and science fantasy. Here you will find the beloved Conan books along with recent titles by the most respected authors in the genre.

☐	10031	NOVA Samuel R. Delany	$1.75
☐	12680	TRITON Samuel R. Delany	$2.25
☐	11718	DHALGREN Samuel R. Delany	$2.25
☐	11950	ROGUE IN SPACE Frederic Brown	$1.75
☐	12018	CONAN THE SWORDSMAN #1 DeCamp & Carter	$1.95
☐	12706	CONAN THE LIBERATOR #2 DeCamp & Carter	$1.95
☐	12031	SKULLS IN THE STARS: Solomon Kane #1 Robert E. Howard	$1.95
☐	11139	THE MICRONAUTS Gordon Williams	$1.95
☐	11276	THE GOLDEN SWORD Janet Morris	$1.95
☐	11418	LOGAN'S WORLD William Nolan	$1.75
☐	11835	DRAGONSINGER Anne McCaffrey	$1.95
☐	12044	DRAGONSONG Anne McCaffrey	$1.95
☐	10879	JONAH KIT Ian Watson	$1.50
☐	12019	KULL Robert E. Howard	$1.95
☐	10779	MAN PLUS Frederik Pohl	$1.95
☐	12269	TIME STORM Gordon R. Dickson	$2.25